The Magical Jewel, A Mystical Knight Novel, Bc
By Jade Stephenson ©.

The Magical Jewel, A Mystical Knight Novel, Book 1.
By Jade Stephenson ©.

Contents

Copyright..1
The Magical Jewel, Prologue.................3
Chapter 1. Unicorn Stables...................4
Chapter 2. The road to Old House...........12
Chapter 3. Tea at Old House.................23
Chapter 4. Shadows in Dark Forest.........34
Chapter 5. Wounded at Old House..........41
Chapter 6. Mystical Knights..................46
Chapter 7. Surprises from the enemy........56
Chapter 8. Magic Training....................69
Chapter 9. Pain from the past................83
Chapter 10. Mirror, Mirror on the wall, Hello
Lucas...95
Chapter 11. Magic Shield....................105
Chapter 12. I hear the voice of my friend...118
Chapter 13. Bad News.......................132
Chapter 14. Goodbye.........................139
Chapter 15. Danger in Dark Forest..........148
Chapter 16. History Lesson..................155
Chapter 17. Trouble Brewing.................163
Chapter 18. Shadows closing in.............168
Chapter 19. Seeing Double..................174
Chapter 20. The Rescue......................181
Chapter 21. Family and Friends.............188
Chapter 22. 1 Month later....................191
Author's Notes..................................195

The Magical Jewel.
A Mystical Knight Novel, Book 1.

Prologue.

Once upon a time in a distant past, darkness came and tried to destroy the light of this world but before the world could be lost it was saved by magic. This magic is now stored in a pointed hexagon shaped jewel that looks purple from a distance but when you look closer you can see every color in existence. It has always been powerful, but too strong for the one who carries it, as it always leads them down a dark path and then disappears.

No one really knows where this jewel came from or how it contains strange magic inside, but one thing is for certain it is looking for the right person to carry it, and when it finally finds them it will want to stay with them forever.

Some people believe that when this happens, they will restore their land to peace once more, but others believe it will never be the same again, it will be the end!!

The Magical Jewel, A Mystical Knight Novel, Book 1.
By Jade Stephenson ©.

Chapter 1.
Unicorn Stables.

"Walk on, good boy." I said to Silver.

Have you ever had that feeling that someone is watching you, so you turn around and there is no one there, well I have had that feeling a lot lately, even now as I ride back to the stables where I live and work.

I know they are many creatures living in Dark Forest, but this feels different, maybe it is just me and I'm being paranoid or maybe someone is watching me, either way I have never had this feeling so strong before. So, I pick up the pace and send my horse Silver into a trot.

We arrived at the end of the forest and ride out into an open field. I live in Greenfield village where there are more fields full of grass, crops, and flowers than any other village around, hence the name. And in the middle of the village is Dark Forest, a forest so thick with trees it can seem dark even with the sun out. Unicorn Stables is situated on the other side of the field, so I send Silver into a canter to get there faster. He surged forward, with his long black tail streaming behind him, his hooves thundered over the ground. I laughed out loud with delight.

Silver is an all-black horse with strands of silver flowing through his mane and tail, he also has silver eyes that is why I named him Silver.

He is the biggest and toughest looking horse at the stables, some people are afraid of him because of his silver eyes as they believe he is connected to the Fairy race or some other magical creature. Whatever he is, he is a great horse and I love him, he has been close with me ever since I rescued him when he was a foal and we have been together ever since.

As we slowed back into a walk and arrive near the gate to exit the field, I hear a voice shouting me. I dismounted off Silver and walked through the gate into the courtyard.
It was Nick my best friend, he walked towards me with a big grin on his face. Great, what kind of trouble was he in now, I thought as I smiled back. He is nineteen years old, four years older than me but he is always acting immature and causing trouble. Even though he does not live with me as he lives with his parents at the village bakery, he grew up with me working with the horses, so I think of him as my brother.

"Hey Rose, how was your ride." Said Nick as he stopped beside me.
"It was great; it's such a lovely afternoon." I replied as I looked up at the bright blue sky.
Nick glanced down at my waist "Damn it Rose you didn't take your dagger with you again."
Every member of the village carries a dagger or some other form of weapon with them while they head through the forest in case one of the monsters living there decides to attack, though they normally stay on the outskirts of the forest closer to the magic realm border and away from people on horses.
"It's fine Nick, anyway Silver can outrun any monster that comes near us, so stop worrying."
"Yeah, well don't let Anthony see you, you won't hear the end of it." Laughed Nick as he ran his hand through his short light brown hair.

We both started walking towards Silver's stable; his stable is the first one you see as you enter the archway leading towards the main house. All the stables are in a large square around a smaller courtyard, with the house at the back. We got inside Silver's stable and started to untack him and give him a rub down with water to cool him down after our long ride.

"So Rose, have you heard the rumors about who's coming to live at the village?" Nick asked as he removed Silver's saddle.

"No, I haven't, who is coming?" I replied and removed his bridle.

"Well Jack heard Helen talking to Hannah about magic users coming here but he didn't hear the whole conversation."

"Well maybe he is mistaken, and miss heard them, why would magic users want to move to this village?"

Magic users are people who can use magic, either by claiming magical items and using the power stored within them or being born with the ability to use magic, like the Shapeshifters or Fairy race. The magic users normally all live in the bigger villages and cities, so they can stick together and look after each other as there has been some trouble in the past with non-magic users claiming they are cursed and dangerous, so it is strange for them to want to move here.

"Nick, Rose, are you in there?" Shouted James as he popped his head over the stable door.

"Yes James we are, what's up?" Laughed Nick as he opened the stable door to let him in.

James is a twelve-year-old boy who likes to act older, he has short blonde hair with brown eyes, and a scar down his left cheek, which helps us tell the difference between him and his twin brother Jack.

"Anthony was looking for you both; he has called for a

meeting we all need to be in his office, now." He said, then stormed off back to the house.

"Ok, what's wrong with him?"

"Well remember, James and Jack hate magic users so if he's heard they are coming, he would be angry." Nick replied.

"Oh yeah your right, but we don't know if the rumors are true yet, he shouldn't worry." I said as I finished taking care of Silver.

"Maybe not but do you blame him." Nick said with a frown.

James and his brother Jack were involved in an accident at the age of five which resulted in the death of their parents, and how James got his scar, it had something to do with magic users, but no one knows the details. They have both hated anything related to magic ever since.

"Come on Rose, we better go to the office." Said Nick as he walked out of Silver's stable carrying his tack.

I said goodbye to Silver and followed Nick to the tack room, which was a small room near the last stable closest to the house. The walls are full of shelves, cupboards, and hooks to store all the horse's tack, rugs, grooming supplies and medical equipment.

"Hey Nick, I haven't seen any empty houses in the village, so where would these magic users live?" I asked as I hung Silver's bridle up on the wall.

"Yeah, that's a good question, I haven't seen any either, well except Old House, but I don't think even magic users would move to that old, haunted house."

Old House is a large, abandoned house on the other side of the forest. No one has lived in there for years, so the path leading up to it is overgrown with weeds and bushes, and the house itself has seen better days. There have been stories of the place being haunted and that is why no one will buy it, but when myself and Nick were kids, we used to play on the swing in the garden, and we never once saw a ghost.

"Well, I am sure magic users can handle it." I said as we both walked to the front door of the house.

The door flew open and out ran Spencer the Unicorn Stables dog, who greeted us both by happily jumping up and wagging his tail. He is a handsome golden cocker spaniel, and he looked playful as always.

Hannah, an eight-year-old girl, and the youngest living at the stables was close behind him, she is a shy girl with long blonde hair and bright blue eyes and is also always full of energy.

"Hello, wait for me Spencer." She shouted then ran off after him into the field before we could reply.

Nick and I smiled then headed into the house. We walked past the reception desk and into the back room where the office is.

It is a large office with filing cabinets and shelves lined with books mostly about horses, along the walls. And in the middle of the room was a large square table where everyone who lives there except Hannah was now sat waiting for us.

Anthony a tall thirty-year-old, with short brown hair and brown eyes was the man in charge of Unicorn Stables; he was sat at the head of the table, reading something with a look of concentration on his face.

Nick and I sat down at the left side of the table next to Jack and James. Sat opposite us was Helen a young woman with long chestnut brown hair and blue eyes; she was Anthony's assistant and girlfriend. She gave us both a smile, but I could tell something was bothering her, but before I could ask her what was wrong, Willow started to talk.

"So, Rose how was Silver on your ride today?"

"He was great as always, he even went and jumped perfectly over some fallen trees." I replied.
"Oh good, but you must be more careful riding in the forest." She said with a smile.
"Don't worry I always am." I smiled back.
Willow Pearl is the one that started up Unicorn Stables; she is also the one who helped raise everyone living here. As she could not have children of her own she took in orphans and abandoned children so Unicorn Stables could go on into the future, she took me in at the age of twelve when my mother passed away due to an unknown illness. Willow is a small, kind, and wise woman who a lot of people go to for advice. After her husband Henry passed away and now that she is seventy-five years old, she has let Anthony be in charge of a lot of decisions concerning the stables, but she still sits with us at meetings.

"Good, everyone is here, now it's time to tell you all why I called this meeting." Said Anthony when he looked away from the papers he was reading.
"Yes, please do." mumbled Helen.
"Some of you may have heard the rumors about magic users coming to live at the village, well I can confirm these rumors are true, they will be moving to Old House." He said, then glanced at Helen.
"Well, they must have been desperate to move if they chose that old place to live." Said Nick.
"Well, everyone knows how stupid magic users can be." Said James in a mad voice.
"Anthony, that's very nice for them but what's it got to do with us?" I asked.
"Well, I'm glad you asked Rose, they will be bringing their horses with them, so we are going to help them settle their horses into their new home."

"What!" Shouted James and stood up.

"James please don't shout; you know Unicorn Stables help all kinds of people and horses." Willow said calmly.

James huffed and sat back down.

Anthony continued talking, "Their horses will be staying in the small yard just outside Old House, but they want us to help them design and build new stables for them, I will be contacting Noah with the details."

Noah Wren is the village builder; he is the one who came up with the idea of teaming up with Unicorn Stables and building horse stables for our village and other villages and towns nearby. He is a strong kind man and if he is not working you usually find him in the village pub having a few drinks. He trained Anthony and Nick to build and when he found out I could draw he showed me how to design the plans for the new stables.

"For this job I want Nick and Rose to be in charge, we will be riding to Old House tomorrow to meet them and have tea while they explain what they want us to do." Explained Anthony.

"I want all of you to give your horses a full groom before you go, we need to give them a good first impression so they will tell their friends about us." Said Willow.

"We don't need any more magic users here." Said Jack, then he got up and stormed out of the office.

I was about to go after him, but his brother beat me to it.

"I'm sure those two will be fine, and once they meet Robert they will realize not all magic users are bad people." Said Willow with a smile.

"Have you met the magic users before, Willow?" I asked.

"Only Robert Odin, on a trip once to Sunlight City, he is a very kind young man who loves animals just as much as you do Rose, so I'm sure you will get along with him."

"Well, if you like him I'm sure I will too." I stood up to leave.

"Alright so myself, Helen, Nick, Rose, Hannah and Noah will be going to Old House tomorrow, I will make sure they all behave themselves." Said Anthony to Willow.

"And I will make sure he stays out of trouble." Said Helen.

"What does that mean, I'm always good." Anthony said with a wink.

Willow laughed "Just make sure you all pay attention and get the job done, but also make new friends and have fun."

"Alright Willow, we will." I said, and then we all left the office.

Chapter 2
The road to Old House.

Running, running, I can't stop running; if I stop or fall down, he will get me!!
The shadows are moving closer, I cannot breathe….
"Aaaah!!!"

There was a large crash, a pain shot up my arm, I opened my eyes and found myself on my bedroom floor, and I looked at my arm and saw a bruise. Ouch, that was one weird nightmare I thought.
"Rose are you alright?" shouted Helen then she opened the door.
Helen's room is right next to mine so if she heard me scream, she is probably worried.
"Yes, I'm alright." I said as I wrapped my blanket around me.
She looked at me as I rubbed my arm. "What happened I heard you scream; wait is that a bruise?"
"I'm fine; I just had a nightmare and fell out of bed." I smiled.
"It must have been bad; do you want to talk about it?"
"No, it's alright, it's not real so it doesn't matter, do you want to talk though, are you sure you will be alright seeing the magic users today?" I said as I placed my jewel around my neck.
After her mother lost her job at a bar that got destroyed by magic users, she left Helen in the care of Willow so she could leave to find more work somewhere new, but she has not been back since, so Helen has never liked magic users as she blames them for breaking up her family.
"I know I'm not keen on magic users and I don't like the sound of this job, but Willow is right, the Unicorn

Stables help all horses and people, no matter who they are, so I will go with everyone today, besides someone has to keep an eye on you." She said.
"What would I do without you?" I smiled back, as she left the room laughing.
Helen always makes me feel better; she is like a big sister and is always looking out for me. I took a deep breath as I started to get dressed into some shorts and a tee-shirt, and I wondered 'why do I keep having these strange dreams?'

Once dressed I walked down the large staircase back towards the reception then turned right and went through the large double doors into the kitchen and dining room.
Everyone who lives here was already out of bed and in the kitchen talking and laughing together like always, even though not all of us are related by blood we have all become a family.
Anthony was making toast while Helen made tea and coffee, the others were already sat at the large table eating. I grabbed some toast off the plate and sat down at the table next to Willow.
"Morning Rose, did you sleep well?" She asked.
"Yes, I slept fine." I lied, as I spread some jam onto my toast, I did not want her to worry.
Helen came over and handed me a hot cup of coffee with a look of concern on her face, she knew I was lying.
"Here Rose, this will help wake you up." Said Helen, then she sat down next to me.
"Thank you." I took a deep breath and inhaled the smell; I have always loved the smell of coffee as it reminds me of my mother who used to drink it all the time.
If Helen knew I have had nightmares nearly every

night she would be even more worried about me.
As Anthony sat down next to Helen he said, "So I
suggest everyone who is going to Old House today
should give your horses a full groom after your
breakfast, the rest of you can clean their horse's tack
then get on with the other jobs that need doing around
the yard, we will leave at 12 o'clock sharp."
After that was said we all ate our breakfast in silence,
I think everyone is nervous about meeting the magic
users today and angry about working with them. I am
more excited; I've never met one before I've only
heard stories about them from my mother.

After breakfast I collected my grooming kit and a
bucket of warm water from the tack room then headed
towards Silver's stable. His head peeped out of the
stable door, and he neighed at me in greeting as I
approached, he looked happy to see me as always. I
opened the stable door and gave him a pat on his
neck.
"Hello boy, lets get you cleaned up."
I've never needed to tie Silver up while I groom him
as we share a close bond, he's normally a good boy
who stands still and he loves the attention.
After I swept the straw out of the way, Silver picked
his heavy hooves up one by one, ready for me to
clean the mud and stones out from under them. After
that was done I picked up my dandy brush and
started to brush the dry mud off his body.
Luckily, the fields have been dry lately so he wasn't
too muddy, in winter all the horses get covered in
mud, so it takes us twice as long to groom them.
Using the bucket of warm water, I got started with
washing Silver's long black tail, when he is clean the
strands of silver hair in his tail and mane sparkle like
stars in the night sky.

As I finished grooming I took a deep breath and listened to the sounds all around me, I could hear birds chirping and flying in the blue sky, I could hear sheep and lambs bleating in the distant fields, bees buzzing in the flowers and the water falling in the fountain. I could also hear my family walking around the yard, talking and emptying buckets of water down drains, today if I listened even harder I could even hear the trees of the forest blowing in the breeze.

Ever since I was little I have always had good hearing but lately it seemed to be getting better and I did not know why.

I patted Silver on his neck and stood back to admire my work.

"There, all clean." I smiled. I on the other hand was covered in horsehair and dust.

Suddenly Silver backed up to the corner of his stable and stamped one of his front hooves to the ground in warning, I turned around and noticed a boy who I have never seen before, ok maybe my hearing is not as good as I thought because I didn't hear him approaching. He looked to be about my age with blue eyes, I could not see the color of his hair as he was wearing a long black cloak despite the warm weather.

"Hello, can I help you with something?" I asked.

He smiled and said, "You can give me the jewel that's around your neck, that would help me."

I looked down at my necklace with a puzzled look then looked back up at the boy "Excuse me?" I said, but he was no longer stood there he was gone.

"Hey, wait!" I shouted then ran out of the stable, he was nowhere in sight, only Anthony and Helen were coming towards me.

"Did you see where that boy went?" I asked them. They both looked at me with confusion.

"What boy? We haven't seen anyone." Helen said looking around.

"I think the heat is getting to you, you're starting to hallucinate." Laughed Anthony.

Helen punched him in the arm.

"Ouch."

"Stop it; it's not even that hot, what boy are you talking about Rose? We only saw you leave the stable." She said.

"I.....Never mind, it doesn't matter." I replied.

Helen looked at me with concern, but before she could say more Anthony asked, "Is Silver all ready to go?"

"Yes, he's all cleaned up." I replied.

They both looked into the stable, "Wow look how handsome he looks." Smiled Helen.

"Good job Rose, now we better get ready too, Jack and James will be tacking up our horses." Said Anthony.

As we walked back towards the house I thought more about the boy as I looked again at the jewel around my neck, did I hear him right? He said he wanted my jewel, but it is nothing special, in fact I only found it a week ago in a field, well Spencer did he sniffed it out for me on one of his morning walks.

It is a long purple hexagon shaped jewel, but I kept it because when you look closer you can see many colors, it sparkled in the sun when I had picked it up and it felt warm.

Once I had got home, I had it cleaned and I attached it onto a silver chain my mother had given me as it matches the bracelet she had given me too, the one my father had given her when they had met. The bracelet has three little charms on it, one of a tiger, one of a heart and one of a fairy. I never knew my father as my mother left him when I was a baby to move to Greenfield village, but she would always speak kindly of him and told me when I was old enough she would tell me more about him and we would meet again one day. She never got that chance as she passed away when I was twelve due to an unknown illness. So the chain and bracelet were special to me, and I would never give them away. Now I even feel connected to the jewel it is like another gift from a member of my family so I will keep it too.

"Hey, Rose are you even listening to me?" Shouted Anthony.

"Oh……Sorry Anthony, what did you say?"

"Wake up Rose, you need to pay attention today go and get dressed we will be leaving soon." He said then marched off.

"Don't worry about him, you know how he gets when we get a new job, but what about you Rose are you sure you're alright?" Asked Helen.

"Yeah, I'm alright just tired, don't worry I will go and get ready." I replied and walked off up the stairs towards my room. I decided to wear a blue checked short sleeved shirt, black jeans, and my black riding boots, they are comfortable to ride in and smart. I also tied my long auburn hair up into a neat plait.

Once dressed I headed back outside to meet with the others, all the horses were stood in the yard fully cleaned and tacked up ready for our journey. Noah was waiting there too as he will be travelling with us through the forest, he spotted me and waved.

"Hello Rose, how are you and Silver today?" He asked.

"We are both good, clean and ready to get to work."

He laughed "Good, I'm glad one of us is ready to work, I could do with another drink everyone else is

on edge it's making me nervous."
"Yes I know, I think it's because we will be working
with magic users." I told him.
"Yes, I think so too." He replied as he rubbed his bald
head anxiously.

Anthony shouted "Alright, everyone saddle up we are
leaving now."
Noah headed towards Fred a large black and white
horse who he enjoyed riding just as much as his
daughter Amy, who came for riding lessons a few
times a week.
Anthony was riding his large black horse Sam; Helen
was on Lady her brown and white mare while Hannah
climbed onto her little black pony Biggles and Nick got
onto his brown horse Murphy.
Now that everyone was ready we all headed through
the gate to the field that led to the forest. Anthony was
in the lead with Helen, Hannah, Noah, Nick and
myself following behind. As we got onto the path that
leads into the forest I could feel Silver starting to get
excited,
"Easy boy we aren't running today." I told him, he
calmed down again and continued to follow Murphy at
a steady pace.
Everyone else was quiet the only sounds I could hear
were the horse's hooves as we walked and the sound
of distant birds singing. I wondered if the others were
also thinking about the magic users and how they
would work with us.
I was not worried I remembered my mother telling me
once not to judge a person just because they are
different, always get to know them first then decide
how you feel about them because you never know
you might end up being the best of friends.
Also, if Willow says this Robert is a good man then

I'm sure the others will be too. As we got further into the forest I could smell the pine trees and wild garlic which always reminded me of my childhood, I smiled remembering the fun times with my mother and the others playing in the forest.

A sudden movement in the trees to my right pulled me out of my memories, and I gently pulled on the reins to tell Silver to stop. I saw it again, it looked like a black shadow of some creature but before I could make out what it was, it disappeared behind some trees.

"Hey, Rose what's wrong?" Shouted Nick.

I looked forward and noticed the others had stopped.

"It's nothing, I just thought I saw something, but I think it has gone now, lets go Silver."

We set off walking again and caught up with the others

"What did you see?" Asked Nick.

"I'm not sure, something black." I replied then turned around in my saddle to have another look behind me but this time there was no creature, there was a boy, the same boy I had seen in front of Silver's stable, standing on the path behind us.

"Hey, it's you." I shouted then turned Silver back around to face him but then he was gone.

"Rose who are you shouting at?" Asked Noah with fear in his voice.

Everyone else had stopped their horses and was now staring at me.

"It was that boy from before he was behind us, but now he's gone." I said as I looked around us.

Helen looked at me with concern, "Rose no one is there, we are the only ones on this path."

"What boy are you talking about?" Asked Nick who was also looking around.

Before I could answer him Anthony interrupted,

"Alright everyone that is enough, we don't have time for this lets get moving, Rose stop messing around."
"I'm not lying I swear to you he was there." I said as I again looked behind me.
Helen looked at Anthony, but he just shrugged his shoulders and told Sam to walk on, the others followed behind him. Before Nick followed, he looked around us once more then said,
"Come on Rose let's go, whoever it was he's gone now." He followed the others over the old stone bridge we had come to.
I took a deep breath and started to follow them, but I was angry, why did this boy keep appearing then running off, what did he want?
And why do I feel like the others don't even believe me?
Before I could think about it more, the others suddenly stopped in front of me, we had arrived at the overgrown path that leads straight to Old House, from here we would be going on foot leading our horses through as we had to also clear the path with the small sickle's and axes we had brought with us.
We dismounted our horses, Anthony, Noah, and Nick led the way clearing the path, cutting through the overgrown bushes, plants, and weeds while Helen and Hannah helped lead their horses behind them. As Silver followed me wherever I went I didn't need to hold his reins, so I took Murphy off Nick and helped lead him through while I also helped trim the side of the path with my sickle.
Helen kept glancing nervously towards Hannah to make sure she was safe, I do not blame her, this path has not been cleared in a while, and we never know what creatures could jump out at us.
As we got further into the forest I suddenly felt a sharp pain on my right arm,

"Ouch." Silver sensed my pain and trotted forward to walk beside me, then he stomped his left foot in warning, he had spotted something in the trees. The other horses also looked agitated.

"Whoa, easy boy it's alright."

I looked through the trees, but I could see nothing hopefully whatever it was, has now left. The horses calmed down, but I noticed Silver was staying by my side to make sure I stayed safe, I patted him on the neck then I looked down at my arm and noticed the deep cut.

"Watch out for those thorns, they're sharp." I warned the others.

Hannah turned around with a puzzled look on her face,

"Um…. But there are no thorns near us Rose." She said.

That is when I noticed we had already made it to the part of the path that was already clear, there were no thorns or bushes around us and there was a gap between me and the trees to my side, there was no way I could have walked into a branch. Before I could figure out what had hurt me, everyone got back on their horses and we set off again down the path, which was now clear for us to ride through, I wondered if the magic users had cleared this part of the path for us.

We finally made it out of the forest, and we could now see Old House, it was a large stone house covered in ivy. The others sent their horses into a trot but before I could follow, I heard someone call my name, it sounded like whoever it was, was behind me so I turned around to look but again there was no one there. Before I could investigate further, I felt Silver pull his head forward, I realized then that the others had already made it to the gate and were now getting

off their horses. Silver did not want to be left behind.
"Alright Silver lets go."
He started to canter so we could catch up with the others and I had a feeling he knew someone was behind us too and he was not happy about it.
We arrived at the gate and slowed to a walk to get through it. The others were standing in the courtyard lined up in a row waiting.
I got off Silver and stood next to Nick,
"What took you so long?" He asked.
I smiled but before I could answer him, we heard someone shouting.
"Hello everyone."

Chapter 3.
Tea at Old House.

A large muscular man stepped out of the door; he looked to be in his early forties with short black hair, a beard, and brown eyes. He looked strong and wise. "You all must be from Unicorn Stables, my name is Robert Odin, though everyone just calls me Odin, it's nice to meet you all."

Others came out of the door behind him, Odin pointed at a tall boy with short blonde hair and blue eyes, who had come out the door first he introduced him. "This is Edmund Myers." He also looked strong, and he looked like he was about the same age as Nick. He smiled and nodded to us all in greeting.

A young woman was stood beside him "Hello everyone I'm Isabella Jones." She said and waved, she was tall and beautiful with long black hair and brown eyes. There was also a young girl who looked to be the same age as me or maybe older, she had long blonde hair but what made me stare was her eyes there were gold.

Another girl came from behind her, and she looked nearly identical, she also had gold eyes, but she was a lot younger maybe eight to ten years old, they must be related. I looked into the little girl's gold eyes and remembered something my mother told me; fairies have gold eyes. Wow I didn't think I would ever get to meet one, fairies liked to stay away from humans and stayed close to their homes.

"This is Marigold May." Said Odin pointing at the older girl, then he pointed at the younger girl and said, "And this young lady is Clover May."

So, they were sisters and with names like those they were definitely fairies.

And last in the lineup was another boy with medium length black hair who looked a little older than me, he was stood further apart from the others and looked like he didn't want to be noticed but he didn't look shy, in fact he looked strong and confident and there was something else about him that made him seem more powerful than the others. When I noticed the color of his eyes I realized why, there were bright green. He was part human and part beast; he was a shapeshifter. When they said magic users were moving to our village they were not kidding, fairies and shapeshifters are the strongest magic users around.

"And over there is Tristan Freeman." Said Odin who pointed at the shapeshifter. He put his hand up and waved but he didn't smile.

Anthony introduced us all one by one to the magic users and Odin came down the line to shake everyone's hand in greeting. He got to me at the end and said. "Hello Rose."

As we shook hands I replied "Hello, it's nice to meet you."

He smiled and was about to walk back to the house but then he suddenly stopped and was staring at me.

"Um......Is there something wrong sir?" Asked Nick who had noticed.

Odin blinked out of the stare "No it doesn't matter......Oh wait your hurt." He said and pointed at my arm. I looked down and saw the blood dripping out of the cut, it looked deeper than I originally thought.

"What happened Rose?" Said Nick with concern.

"It's alright; I think I just cut myself while riding through the forest." I told him.

"Tristan, come here." Odin shouted.

Tristan walked over to us. "Take Rose to my office and help her bandage her arm." Said Odin.

Tristan glanced at me then looked at Nick who looked annoyed.

"It's alright just point me in the direction of your bathroom, and I will clean myself up." I said.

"Nonsense, you are our guests we need to look after you, Tristan please help her." Said Odin.

"Yeah alright, follow me." Tristan said, but before he walked off back into the house Odin whispered something in his ear, I didn't catch what he said as Nick coughed beside me but whatever he said Tristan looked shocked then he looked back at me with a strange look in his eyes.

"The rest of you can follow me I will show you a place where you can put the horses before we eat." Said Odin, he walked off heading towards the back of the house while talking to Anthony, the others started to follow. I handed Silver's reins over to Nick then followed Tristan inside the house.

We passed through the large brown wooden doors and into the entrance hall, the first thing I noticed was the smell, but it was not an unpleasant smell, it was a musty old smell with a hint of coffee and flowers. I also noticed the old paintings of the people who lived here long ago still hanging on the walls and in one corner many boxes and bags were stacked up high, the magic users still needed to do more work before they could call this place their home.

We walked past the large staircase and entered the first door on the left, so this is Odin's office, I thought as I looked around in wonder at the many objects. One wall had a large bookcase filled with many books, wooden filing cabinets stood next to a black leather sofa and a small table next to that had a model of a castle. On the far wall was the large double window looking out at the garden. And in the middle of the room was a large desk with lots of papers, maps and scrolls, there was a large chair at one side of the desk and two smaller ones on the opposite side.

Tristan walked up to one of the chairs and pointed at it, "Take a seat, I will go and find the medical kit." He said then walked back out the door.

I sat down and while I waited I took a closer look at the desk; I noticed a photograph in a brown wooden frame decorated with painted on flowers. I picked up the frame and looked closer, it was a photo of the magic users I had just met all stood together smiling looking incredibly happy in front of a large waterfall but there was also another boy with them who I hadn't met standing next to Tristan with his arm around his neck laughing. I wondered if I would get to meet him, he looks like Tristan maybe they are related.

I put the photo down and spotted a wooden model of a large black cat, so I picked it up to take a closer look, it was stunning and looked alive it even had bright green eyes. It looked more like a panther then a normal sized cat. I was still holding it when Tristan came back into the room carrying a green medical box; he stopped when he saw what I was holding.

"Sorry I was just having a look; it is very well made." I said as I placed it back on the desk. He took the seat opposite me and smiled as he put the medical kit down to open it.

"It's alright, I'm glad you like it, my brother made it."

"Did he move here with you?" I asked.

"No……He died last year." He said as he pulled the bandages from the box.

"Oh, I'm sorry." I looked at the photo and wondered if the boy who I hadn't met was his brother.

I understand now why Tristan has a sad look in his eyes, his heart was still broken, and it may never heal, it hurts losing the ones you care about, I know that. I flinched, a sharp pain shot across my arm I looked back at Tristan with concern, he held a cloth in his hands which he must have used to wipe the cut on my arm, it stung.

"Sorry, the wound needed cleaning first, it's deep but it doesn't need stitches, are you sure a thorn did this?" He asked.

"I think so, or a sharp tree branch, what else could it have been?"

"It doesn't matter." He started to wrap the bandage around my arm; we sat in silence as he worked. I took hold of the jewel around my neck and looked out of the window; the garden was still overgrown with many plants, but I could still see the old stone bird bath where a few little birds perched on the edge. I looked back at Tristan and noticed he had finished with my arm, but he was staring at my neck.

"What's wrong?" I asked.

"Um.….Nothing, I have finished, we better get back to the others." He said as he glanced back down at my necklace before getting up and walking to the door. I know it's pretty, but a lot of people seemed interested in my jewel lately, I wonder if that other boy I keep seeing came with the magic users. I shrugged my shoulders and hurried off after Tristan, he had bandaged my arm well, he must have had some first aid training.

"Thank you, Tristan." I said as we walked back through the house. He nodded and pushed open the large door we had arrived at, it led to the large kitchen where everyone was gathered around a large table full of food.

Helen walked over to me, glanced nervously at Tristan, and asked, "Are you alright Rose?"

I could tell she was worried I had been alone with a

magic user, and Tristan had also noticed the fear in her eyes, but he didn't look angry just sad, so I replied, "Yes I'm fine, Tristan helped me."
"Oh…..Ok good." She said then walked back to the table and sat down next to Hannah and Anthony. Tristan sighed then went to the opposite side of the table to sit next to Odin. I noticed Nick on the same side of the table, he waved and pointed to the empty seat between himself and Tristan then he gave me a thumbs up sign with a big grin on his face. I shook my head and smiled then went and sat down next to him. I looked around the kitchen and noticed the only thing that had changed were the large double glass doors leading into the garden, they had put up newer ones as the old ones had been fallen apart for years, they had kept the old cookers and the stone bread oven was still on the wall but the kitchen had been cleaned and new indoor plants and herbs had been put into the pots so the whole room felt new and looked great. As everyone else took a seat at the table, Odin stood up and said,
"I would like to thank you all for coming and helping us with our horses, I hope we will all become good friends, please help yourself to the food it's very good, Marigold and Clover made it."
He sat back down and started grabbing the food off the plates in the middle of the table to put on his, and then he started eating a sandwich. I looked down at the table there was a lot of food, different flavored sandwiches, crackers, rice balls, fruit, vegetables, and cakes too. Each plate had a label telling us what was on it, so we knew what we were eating, everything looked and smelled delicious. Everyone else started helping themselves to food, so I grabbed a few cheese and salad wraps and took a bite. Yum these are nice; I happily ate the rest in silence while I

watched the others enjoy their food and talk. I noticed Nick was stuffing his mouth with rice balls and making Marigold and Clover laugh. I smiled; Nick has always been good at making new friends. Anthony and Noah were talking to Odin, but Helen and Hannah didn't look too happy about it, I suppose it will take them longer to trust the magic users.

I spotted some little apple pies, so I put my hand out to grab one but at the same time so did Tristan, so we ended up grabbing each other's hands instead.

"Sorry." I said.

He grabbed an apple pie and held it out to me "Here." he said, then he took one for himself and started eating.

"Thanks." I replied and took a bite out of mine.

I heard Odin laugh so I looked up and noticed he was watching me and Tristan. "It looks like we have found someone who likes apple pies just as much as you do Tristan." He said.

Tristan frowned at him and grabbed another cake.

"So Rose I noticed your horse Silver looks different than the others and Anthony told me you saved his life when he was a foal, why don't you tell us what happened." Odin said.

"Um....Ok." I took another sip of my orange juice before I told the story.

"When we were little my mother, Nicks parents and Willow took myself, Nick, Helen, and Anthony on a picnic in the forest not too far from here. And I decided to go and explore by myself, I had a bad habit of wandering off on my own." I explained.

"Had a bad habit, you still do that." Laughed Nick.

I smiled "Well maybe a little, so after a while of walking about by myself I heard a man's voice behind some trees so I went to take a look and saw a large wagon being pulled by a large ox, it had stopped as a man was behind it whipping a young foal trying to get it onto the wagon, I could tell he was hurt and didn't want to go with him, so I did what anyone would do, I ran in front of the man and blocked him from whipping the foal again, then told the man to stop it and leave." I finished and took another sip of my drink.

"Not anyone would have done that, she was only seven and she left out the part about being whipped herself, she still has the mark on her hand and when she still wouldn't leave, the man pulled out a knife luckily that's when we arrived, Rose's mother pulled out her own knife and shouted, 'get away from my daughter' which scared the man, he jumped on his wagon and rode off never to be seen again." Said Anthony who smiled at me.

"Yeah, Rose's mother kept her away from the forest for a while after that, but she didn't mind as she spent all her time with Silver taking care of him." Nick told the others.

I smiled and looked down at the sharp line you could still see on my hand, it hurt like hell when the man had whipped me, but I wouldn't change how I acted that day, I would give my life to save Silvers.

"Well, that was a brave thing to do, I bet your mother is proud and she sounds like a caring person, is she at Unicorn Stables too? I would like to meet her." Said Odin.

I shook my head sadly and Helen replied, "Sadly she passed away when Rose was twelve, but you're right she was a great woman who we all miss a lot, Willow took Rose in, and we have all grown up together and become a family and no one will break us up." She smiled at me when I looked up at her, I was glad she told them, she knew it was hard for me to talk about my mother sometimes.

Odin smiled at me and said, "I'm sorry Rose it sounds

like you have had some difficult times in your life but I'm glad you have found a new family and I bet Silver is grateful too."

"Yeah, I bet he is, we have seen horses before that look like Silver, they live in the Fairy Nation." Explained Isabella.

"Wow, really?" I asked and looked at the magic users with keen interest.

Odin laughed "Yes they live among the Fairy Folk but it's rare to see anyone ride them, in fact only the royal fairies have ever ridden one and even that is a rare sight now."

"Well, that doesn't surprise me much, Rose has always had a way with animals, she can understand them better than any of us." Said Noah.

I blushed "My mother said I got that from my father."

"Well, that is a great gift, Odin is right it is rare, these horses are known to be the wildest and strongest you will come across. The fairies call them the horse masters, isn't that right Marigold?" Said Isabella.

"Yes, there were a few problems in the past with some non-magic users taking them away from their herds and trying to sell them in different lands to make a profit, so you are both lucky you found each other." Smiled Marigold.

"Maybe one day, me and Silver can meet the other horses that look like him, I think he would like that." I said and smiled back.

"Yes, maybe you will get the chance one day." Odin stood up, "Though for now I think it's time we went outside so I can show you all where we want the stables to be built."

We all got up and walked out of the glass doors and into the garden, there was a lot of long grass, wildflowers, bushes, and a few small apple trees all around us. You could smell all the different scents that came from them and hear the bees buzzing as they flew around the flowers. Nick sneezed as the strong pollen affected his nose. We left the garden and walked around to the side of the house, then we entered through a gate into a large square area that had fencing all around. The fencing needed repairing and there were a lot of weeds and broken bricks that needed clearing out but under our feet were flat stone slabs so it should be a suitable place to build our wooden stables.

"So, this is where we would like the stables to go, as you can see it needs a lot of work before the place is ready for you to build them but of course we will help wherever we can." Said Odin.

"Yes, this area looks good I'm sure we won't have any trouble building them here." Said Noah as he looked around.

Odin, Noah, and Anthony walked off to inspect the fence and the rest of the area, while they talked the rest of us stood and watched. As we waited, I took out my small sketch pad and pencil from my pouch that was attached to my belt and started to draw a rough design of the area.

As I was drawing, I noticed the others had gone quiet, so I looked up and noticed them watching Odin shaking the broken fence as he laughed but I also noticed Isabella and Tristan were watching me draw, I smiled at them then finished my picture.

After a while Odin, Noah and Anthony came back to join us.

"Well, it's time for us to get back, we have discussed some ideas, but Nick and Rose can come back here tomorrow and take some measurements and start clearing the area. Also Rose you can draw some more designs." Explained Anthony.

I nodded and Nick said, "Right Boss."
We walked back to the front of the house where our horses were tied up waiting for us in the small field. Once they were all tacked up and ready to go, we all mounted up. Before we left to go Odin said,
"Thank you for coming, it was nice to meet you all, we will look forward to working with you and please send my regards to Willow."
We all waved and said goodbye then set off back down the track towards the forest to head back home.

Chapter 4.
Shadows in Dark Forest.

Today I will be starting work at Old House with Nick. I was to meet him at his house in the village so we can both ride through the forest on the shorter path, we won't be taking our horses today but our bicycles.
I had already gone through the forest by myself to get to the village, but I had felt uneasy and worried. I don't know why, I grew up playing in the forest and I have never felt this way before, but lately something feels different, something has changed.
I pedaled through the village, our village is not as large as others, it has a few old stone houses and a little shop that sells food and other supplies, next to that was the bakery. There was a pub, a village hall where meetings and other events took place. And towards the end of the village was the farm and flower shop and next to that was the Horse house and arena where our horse events took place, the Horse house was a small building where the riders would get ready for the shows and behind that were the stables.
In the center of it all was the large stone fountain with two stone fish in the middle that I went past to head towards the bakery where Nick lived with his parents.

"Hey Rose, what took you so long?" Shouted Nick as I stopped in front of the bakery and climbed off my bike, Nick's mother was also stood waiting.
"Hello Nick, hello Rachel."
"Hello Rose, are you feeling alright? You look a little pale." Said Rachel Wilson.
"Yeah, I'm alright." I lied but I didn't want to tell them I have had bad dreams all week and I kept thinking someone was following me all the way here, I didn't

want to worry them. I took my bottle of water out of my bag and took a sip.

"Well alright but don't work too hard today, Nick you better look after her and be careful near those magic users, here I have made them some cakes." She said then passed the box she was holding to Nick, who took it and peeped inside.

"Have you added poison to them?" Nick said with a laugh.

His mother slapped him on the top of his head,

"No, don't say such things, you know our shop needs customers even if they are magic users, now hurry up and get to work." With that said she stormed off back into the bakery to help her husband with a customer.

"You deserved that." I smiled and took the box from Nick who was rubbing his head, I looked inside and as usual the cakes looked and smelled delicious.

I looked into the window of the bakery and watched Nick's parents set up little tables for the customers who would go in and sit down to enjoy their food.

Mr. Wilson saw me, he smiled and waved, and I waved back.

"So, are you ready to go?" I asked Nick.

"Yes, let's get moving before my mother asks us to do something else." He said and climbed onto his bike.

I placed the box of cakes in the basket I have on the front of my bike, and then strapped my bag onto my shoulders then followed Nick back through the village.

As we cycled passed the fish fountain Nick stopped.

"What's wrong?" I asked.

"I was going to ask you that, I know you better, so you can't fool me like my mother, I know you were lying when you told her nothing was wrong with you." He said with a concerned look on his face.

"Nick I'm alright really, I think I'm just tired I didn't sleep well last night that's all, so come on let's go." I

said then started to pedal my bike again and headed
onto the path that led to the forest.
"Fine." Said Nick then he followed me.
I took a deep breath and inhaled the smell of pine and
oak trees all around us, we rode down the path in
silence for a while but then Nick suddenly stopped.
"Did you hear that?" He asked looking around us.
Oh, good so it wasn't just me hearing things.
"Um.....Yes, what was it?" I asked him.
"I don't know, it sounded like someone was banging
drums or something."
Suddenly darkness surrounded us, and the air grew
thick, I looked at Nick but before I could say
something he pointed at my neck with a weird look on
his face. I looked down and noticed the jewel on my
necklace was glowing a bright yellow. I gasped in
surprise, what on earth is happing I thought.
"Rose what is going on?" shouted Nick.
I shook my head but before I could reply a powerful
force knocked us both off our bikes; we both yelled
out and tumbled over some tree roots. The air had
been pushed out of my lungs and it hurt to breathe
but I had to get up, I had to help Nick. When I looked
towards him he was standing and holding his knife,
damn I had left mine at home again, I spotted a large
stick, so I grabbed it and we both stood back-to-back.
"Nick! What was that?" I yelled.
"I don't know, I didn't see anything, come on we have
to get out of here." He grabbed my arm and pulled me
back towards our bikes, but they were too damaged
to ride so we left them and started running in the
direction of Old House.
As we ran strange dark figures with red eyes started
to appear from behind the trees, they moved like
shadows in twilight, and they were closing in. We ran
over the small bridge to the other side, but the

shadows were fast.

One got close to Nick who was running in front of me.

"Nick, look out!" I yelled, but it was too late, it pounced onto Nick.

They both tumbled to the floor fighting each other, and the other shadows circled around me, I became surrounded, and I could no longer see Nick. My heart skipped a beat I had never seen creatures like this before they made me feel cold and alone, fear welled up inside me as I noticed their sharp fangs and claws, but the worst thing was the blood leaking from their red eyes.

My hands started to shake as I held the stick tighter, I did not know what to do, they were just standing there staring at me.

I knew I had to think of something, come up with a plan to escape but before I could, someone else appeared out of the darkness, it was a boy.

"Hello Rose, it's nice to see you again." He said.

I couldn't believe it; he was the boy from before, the one who appeared at the stables and in the forest and he had even been in my nightmares.

"Who are you? What do you want?" I asked with my voice shaking.

"Why Rose, don't be scared, my name is Finn and I have come to take your jewel, my pets won't attack you, well not yet anyway." He laughed.

I took a deep breath and asked, "Why do you want this jewel?"

"It's pretty and I want it, it doesn't belong to you so hand it over and maybe your friend won't get hurt anymore." He said as the creatures around us moved away so I could see Nick; he was lying on the floor with his eyes shut.

"Nick!" I shouted but he did not move.

"Give me the jewel and I will leave you and your friend

alone." Said Finn smiling.

I took hold of my necklace to remove it from my neck but before I could I heard a voice say,

"Don't do it Rose, if he gets the jewel everyone will be in danger."

"No." I said.

"Then your friend will die!" Shouted Finn.

A shadow moved towards Nick.

"Noooo!" I screamed and threw the stick I was holding towards it, but as I did a large blue light appeared out of my hand and also flew towards the shadow. It was like lightning, all the creatures moved away from me and Nick as though they were scared, the darkness faded and the air cleared, but I felt weak.

I managed to run to Nick's side "Nick, wake up." I cried.

I looked up and saw Finn coming towards me with an evil gleam in his eyes.

"So, you can use the magic." He said angrily.

I got up and grabbed Nick's knife and held it in front of me pointing it towards Finn. I had no choice but to stand and fight.

"I'm warning you, stay away from us or else."

Finn laughed "Are you threatening me? You have no idea who you are dealing with, but you have guts this is going to be fun."

He moved closer but then he suddenly stopped as a loud roar sounded from behind me. I quickly jumped to the other side of Nick so I could look behind me but still keep an eye on Finn, this could be some kind of trick, but Finn looked scared, and he was backing off. I did not blame him as behind me a large black panther was moving through the trees towards us.

His bright green eyes were shining in the darkness, and he looked angry. I glanced towards Finn and noticed he was now holding a sword; the shadows had moved closer to him and also looked like they were now carrying weapons of some kind.

I gulped, what the hell was I going to do now? I would not stand a chance against swords and a panther. I heard the voice again.

"**Don't worry the panther is on your side**." It said.

I looked around me, but I couldn't see anyone else, who was that? I wondered.

The panther had moved closer, so I pointed the knife towards it hoping I didn't need to use it, the panther glanced at me then walked straight passed. It stalked towards Finn.

"So, the Mystical Knights have joined the party, be careful or it will end like last time." Said Finn.

The panther snarled at him, Finn laughed and disappeared behind the shadows as they started moving towards us. The panther roared then leaped forward to attack. I suddenly heard horses running towards me; I turned around and saw Odin and Edmund riding down the path with swords in their hands.

They jumped off their horses and ran towards me; Odin shouted "Rose, look out."

I turned and saw a shadow thrust its sword towards me, I dodged out of the way and put the knife up as it swung its sword towards me again, another bolt of blue light flashed in front of me, and the shadow disappeared. I started to feel dizzy, and I dropped to my knees out of breath.

"Tristan stay near Rose; we will take care of the rest." Shouted Edmund as he and Odin ran past me to join the fight.

Wait, where was Tristan? I thought as I looked around.

The panther came back over to my side, I pointed the knife back towards him, but he just stared at me with its bright green eyes.

Wait! "Tristan?" I asked.

The panther came closer and bowed its head. No way, this panther was Tristan, wow that is crazy, so he was a shapeshifter.

I took a deep breath and pulled myself up then I grabbed hold of Nick's arms and pulled him to a fallen tree nearby, so he was more protected, he was still breathing but we needed to get him to a doctor. I looked back to Odin and Edmund who was still fighting the strange creatures. Odin had a sword that kept firing some kind of yellow light every time it hit a shadow, it looked like lightning bolts. And Edmund was somehow throwing fire balls out of his hands, what the hell was going on around here, I thought and glanced back at Tristan who was still near me.

More shadows appeared around us, I stood back up to protect Nick, Tristan roared and started to fight them off as they got closer. A few were coming too close to Nick, so I shouted,

"Stay away!" And threw my hands up, somehow a large blue light flew out of the jewel around my neck and started hitting the shadows, one by one they disappeared.

Odin, Edmund, and Tristan looked towards me with concern.

I started to feel dizzy, and I felt my body start to fall, I had no control and the world turned black.

Chapter 5.
Wounded at Old House.

I was in Dark Forest with shadows and wolves all around me, their eyes were burning red, and I was too scared to move. Then from behind the shadows a young man appeared, I could not make out his features as he wore a black cloak with a large hood that covered his head. He held out his hand and took mine. "Do not trust the people you are with now, they want the jewel for themselves, I want it to make the world a better place, to save everyone, I will let you help me, but you must leave the family living at Old House." He said as he tried to touch the jewel around my neck. I heard a loud roar.

I opened my eyes I was in an unknown bed, I quickly sat up and when the room stopped spinning, I took in my surroundings. The first thing I noticed was the second bed next to mine, and in that bed was a sleeping Nick. I climbed off the bed and noticed my hand had been bandaged up, I must have injured it when I fell off my bike, I also felt the bruises on my ribs. Ouch!
I walked towards the bed Nick was in to make sure he was alright, he had a nasty looking bruise on his head and a bandage wrapped around his arm, tears welled up in my eyes as I remembered him trying to protect me. I took a deep breath and had another look around the room, it was a small room with the two beds and shelves along the wall lined with more wooden animals like the panther Tristan's brother had made.
I quickly moved to the window and looked out, I recognized the overgrown garden and nearby forest, we were at Old House.

I knew it would be best to leave Nick rest while I found out what was going on around here, so I walked to the door and tried the handle, to my relief it was unlocked, so I wasn't a prisoner, that's good.

I walked out the room and headed down the corridor towards the stairs, no one was around but as I got to the bottom of the stairs I could hear shouting.
"You must have known she had that thing, why the hell didn't you take it off her or warn her so she would be more careful, and then maybe they wouldn't have got hurt."
I recognized that voice; it belonged to Nick's mother. I got to the door of Odin's office, but I didn't open it as I heard another voice I knew.
"Now Rachel I'm sure they did everything they could to help, and Doctor Thomas did say they were both going to be alright." Said Willow.
"Yes, with plenty of rest they both should be fine." Said Doctor Thomas.
"Rose is not going to be fine; she's been having nightmares for weeks and seeing things, you need to take that thing off her neck now!" Shouted Helen.
I looked down at my necklace and took a deep breath, 'what is this thing?' I thought.
"We will do what we can to help her, but removing the jewel won't change anything, she is connected to it now." Said Odin.
It was time I found out for myself what was going on so I took the jewel from around my neck and put it in my pocket that way everyone will be happy, then I opened the door. Everyone in the room turned to face me as I entered.
"Rose, are you alright?" Shouted Helen who ran to me and gave me a hug.
"Um…Yeah I'm alright, don't worry." I said as I

hugged her back.

I let go of her and looked at everyone else, Willow smiled and said,

"I'm glad you're safe dear."

I nodded and smiled back then looked at the doctor and asked, "Doctor is Nick going to be alright?"

He pushed his glasses up his nose, scratched his short brown beard, and replied with a smile "Yes, don't worry about him it looks worse than it is, and you know Nick, he will be annoying you again in no time."

Doctor Thomas is the only doctor in the village he is very kind and a great doctor, so I knew he was telling the truth.

I looked at the others in the room, all the magic users smiled at me, but I saw concern in their eyes.

"Rose I am glad to see you back on your feet; I assume you have a few questions for us but…" He was about to say more but he noticed Tristan moving towards me.

"Where has the jewel gone?" Tristan growled as he grabbed my arm, he had noticed it was missing from around my neck.

I flinched and pulled my arm back.

"Get away from her!" Shouted Helen who stood between us.

Nick's parents moved closer, and Willow stood up from her chair and said, "Helen calm down."

I looked back at Tristan, and I saw regret and pain in his eyes, the magic users had helped me and Nick, so the least I could do was hear what they had to say, I still needed to know what had happened in the forest. I wasn't sure if I could fully trust them, but I had to try, so I took the jewel from my pocket and held it up.

"It's fine I still have it." It started to glow again, when I looked at the others I saw fear in their eyes, so I quickly put it away again and said "I…. Um thank you everyone for helping me and Nick. And yes I would like some answers." I looked at Odin.

He smiled and said "Of course, and don't worry Rose we won't let anyone else hurt you." He looked at the others in the room. "I think it would be best if we talked with Rose alone."

"I don't think that's wise." Said Mr. Wilson who had been stood quietly since I entered the room.

Before Odin said something, Willow spoke up, "It's fine Matthew, I think Robert is right, it would be best, she needs to learn the truth herself, lets go back to Unicorn stables and wait for her to return." Willow placed her arm on Helen's shoulder then looked at me, I nodded.

"Alright, I don't like it, but she is under your care, we will be taking our son back with us in the cart." Rachel said then hugged me before she left the room. Her husband followed her along with Doctor Thomas and Willow, before Helen followed them she hugged me again and whispered in my ear "Be careful."

"I will escort them back home to make sure they stay safe." Said Marigold who left with Clover.

Isabella came over to my side and said, "Come on lets all go and sit in the kitchen and I can make you some hot chocolate if you like." I smiled then nodded and followed her and the other magic users out the door and down the corridor towards the kitchen.

Before I entered the kitchen I noticed Doctor Thomas and Nick's father carrying Nick on a stretcher out the front door, I watched them leave. I swallowed a lump in my throat and clenched my hands into fists, I was angry and sad, I hope Nick wakes up soon.

I shut the front door behind them and turned to follow the magic users into the kitchen, but they had already gone; only Tristan stood behind me and he said.

44

"I'm sorry about before, I didn't mean to scare you, and don't worry about Nick the only reason he hasn't woken up yet is because he's low on energy after fighting the shadows, he will be fine after he gets plenty of rest."

I smiled at him and said, "It's alright, thank you for rescuing us… and um…were you that panther in the forest?"

"Yes." He replied and opened the door to the kitchen.

"Cool." I said.

He looked back at me and smiled.

Chapter 6.
Mystical Knights.

We all took a seat around the table with a cup of hot chocolate. Odin began to talk. "So, Rose before I begin to explain things to you, I will first ask you a question, have you heard about the Mystical Knights?"

"Yes of course, they help protect the shapeshifter king at Sunlight City, right?" I replied.

"Yes, that's right but that's not all they do, they also locate and find magical objects, take them to Sunlight City and keep them safe, that is why we are here as we are part of the Mystical Knight Guild." He took a sip from his cup then continued. "The Fairy nation has a way of knowing where magical objects appear, but they can't always tell you the exact location or what the object looks like only the closest area the object is near, so we as Mystical Knights travel to villages, forests and different lands searching for those magical objects to take back home if we can. Sometimes though other people find them first, when that happens we can normally buy the object off them, but sometimes we can't."

He drank some more out of his cup, so my jewel is a magical object I should have noticed that when it started glowing, I am such an idiot. My mother used to tell me stories of the Mystical Knights collecting magic; this must have been what she meant, so it was true.

I took the jewel from my pocket and held it up over the table towards Odin. "Well, if it's that important to you then you should have it, I only found it in a field, well the dog did, you should have told me you needed it." I said.

Odin looked surprised then he smiled sadly.

"I'm afraid with that particular jewel, things aren't that simple." Said Isabelle who was sat next to Odin.

"What do you mean?" I asked confused, why couldn't they just take it?

"Well, it's a little hard to explain but sometimes we find rare magical objects different from the rest, these objects connect to the person who carries it and only that person can use it and taking it away from them is hard and sometimes impossible. The jewel you carry is one, maybe we should demonstrate. Rose give the jewel to Tristan." Said Odin.

I looked beside me at Tristan, he held out his hand, so I placed the jewel in it. He then got up and left the room, I looked at the others even more confused.

We sat in silence then Tristan walked back into the room and sat down, the jewel was not in his hand.

"Um.....I don't get it." I said.

"I think that's enough time, Rose check your pocket." Said Isabella.

I didn't know what was going on, but I did what she said, and I felt something.

"No way, that's impossible." I said, startled at what had just happened. I then took the jewel from my pocket; my hand was shaking.

"That's magic." Laughed Edmund.

"Are you sure you can't just take it somehow?" I asked.

"Well, there is another way you can try to give us the jewel, but it has only worked once." Said Odin.

"Ok what do I need to do?" I asked.

"You have to break the link with the jewel by using your blood to cancel the contract between you, but you have to be willing to make that choice and trust that giving us the jewel is a good idea. Also, it is

47

believed that if the jewel doesn't want to leave you, it won't. Like I said before it has only worked once and sadly that plan didn't work out too well."

"Alright I will try, I believe the jewel is better off with someone who knows more about magic, can you show me how to do it?" I replied.

Odin nodded and passed me his dagger, "You need to cut your hand and place a small amount of your blood onto the jewel then repeat these words 'I Rose, will grant you permission to take the jewel, please jewel be with the Mystical Knights.' The jewel will then leave you, but only if it wants to."

I nodded cut my thumb and dropped some blood onto the jewel then I repeated what he had said. The jewel lit up a bright green, rose above the table between us and then floated back towards me and landed on the table in front of me.

"So did it work, can you take it now?" I asked.

"No, I'm sorry Rose, I'm afraid this means you and that jewel are connected now and there is no going back. You are responsible for keeping it safe and away from people who would use it to inflict harm to the innocent, you will need to learn how to control the magic stored inside but don't worry we will help you." Explained Odin.

"Don't worry! I have just been attacked by a weirdo called Finn who has pet shadows, Nick could have been killed, and now I can't even give this jewel away and you tell me not to worry, that doesn't really help you know." I said angrily as I wiped my thumb with a tissue Isabella had given me.

"We understand Rose, this is a lot to take in and it's hard when you're not used to living around magic, we will all help you the best we can, but we understand if you need some time to think about it." Isabella said with a calming voice.

I took a deep breath and said.

"Sorry, I'm alright but something doesn't make sense, if what you say is true about the jewel being difficult to take off me then why was Finn trying so hard to get his hands on it, doesn't he know? Maybe we should explain to him why he can't have it."

"Oh, he knows alright, the only way to take it from you is to kill you or make you one of them." Said Edmund.

"Edmund!" Shouted Odin.

"What? She asked." He replied.

"He could also have been trying to make you break the contract like we have just tried." Said Isabella.

"Then why didn't he? I mean he just kept asking for the jewel, and he didn't tell me how to break the contract, he also had plenty of chances to….to kill me, so why didn't he?" I asked and looked around the table at the confused faces.

"She's right, something doesn't add up, maybe they were trying to get her to join them, or we are missing something." Odin said as he looked at the jewel I had put on the table.

"They know she can use the magic inside now, so maybe they will try to make her join them." Said Isabella.

"Join them, what do you mean?" I asked with concern, that didn't sound good, in fact none of this was sounding good.

"Well, there have been some cases where people with magical objects have decided to join the Dark Shadow Guild. That guild is full of bad people who will stop at nothing to get what they want even if it means hurting others. No one knows who the official leader of the group is but whoever it is wants to rule over all the lands. Finn is a part of that guild; they can also control the shadow demons which you witnessed. Once someone with a magical object joins them, they can use that power to help with their plans." Explained Odin.

I nodded as I drank some more hot chocolate, I thought about what he said. So those monsters in the forest were called shadow demons, makes sense but something did not so I said.

"Well, he was threatening to kill Nick so if he wanted me to join him he wasn't doing it the right way now was he."

There was silence around the room as the others were thinking, then Tristan finally spoke "There is another reason that you all aren't thinking about, the rumors could be true about them finding another way to take the jewel, the box."

"Damn, if that's true we could be in more danger then we thought." Said Odin.

"A box?" I asked.

Isabella answered, "There have been rumors about the Dark Shadow Guild building or finding some kind of box that can take magical objects away from the original owner by force, and stop that object from disappearing, they would be able to use the magic stored within them, but that's just a rumor surely it's not true." She looked at Odin.

"Tristan has a point though, they aren't going to kill Rose because once she's dead the jewel will disappear and the search will start all over again, and if they were threatening Nick maybe they don't want her to join them so that leaves the third option, they have the box." Said Edmund.

The room went very quiet as they thought about what Edmund had just said.

"So basically, I have a magical jewel that a Dark Shadow Guild wants, and they will stop at nothing to get it and if they succeed it will be bad for everyone, and I am the only one that can use it and stop them?"

This was not sounding very good at all, I thought.
"Yes, that about sums it up, but like I said before we
are all here to help you." Smiled Odin.
These Mystical Knights seem like nice people but for
some reason I still felt as though they were hiding
something from me and something important. I stood
up.
"I need some air." I said. I picked up the jewel, put it in
my pocket then left the room quickly before anyone
could stop me.
Once I was outside and behind the house I took a
deep breath. I looked around me at the trees and then
looked up to the sky, it already felt like it was getting
late I must have been sleeping longer than I thought. I
sat down on the lush green grass; I needed to think
and work out what to do next. I wondered could I
really trust the Mystical Knights. I took the jewel from
my pocket, this was meant to hold magic, but it just
looked like a normal jewel to me, the only reason I
had picked it up was because Spencer had found it
and it looked pretty. Though maybe that was not the
only reason I had picked it up, maybe I was meant to
have it, I do feel some kind of connection to it and
now that I think about it the jewel has always felt
warm as though it were alive. I took another deep
breath and placed the jewel back around my neck, I
should probably keep this thing close for now. I knew
the first thing I needed to do was head back home to
Unicorn Stables and make sure my family was safe,
then ask Willow for some advice I am sure she will
know what to do.

I got up to walk away but as I did I noticed some dead
flowers nearby, it made me feel sad, suddenly the
jewel around my neck began to glow a bright green
color again, I gasped what should I do now. The

green light expanded and touched the grass then one by one flowers started to grow all around me. Wow, I thought, was this really the true magic of the jewel, it didn't feel bad. I laughed in delight as more flowers grew; it was making me feel happy again.

"Rose!" I spun around and the glowing light stopped, I suddenly felt dizzy. It was Tristan who had shouted, and he quickly came to stand beside me, he put his hand on my arm as he noticed me lose my balance.

"Are you alright? You have to be more careful, using too much magic when you're not used to it can drain your energy." He said.

"I'm fine." I lied.

"Let's go back to the house, you need more rest." He looked around his feet at all the flowers and looked concerned, which did not help me feel any better, did I do something wrong? I thought.

When we got back to the house Isabella was waiting outside for us. "I hope you're feeling better now Rose, if you want to talk more or ask any more questions your welcome to come back inside and we will help you the best we can." She said.

"Um thank you, I was wondering did you bring our bikes back or are they still in the forest?" I asked.

"Oh yes we managed to get them for you we put them in the shed at the side of the house but I'm afraid they are damaged and the box of cakes you had were flattened" She explained.

I rubbed my eyes and yawned I suddenly felt very tired, "Ok thanks, I will go and have a look."

I quickly walked off and headed towards the shed but before I went inside I turned around to make sure I wasn't followed; I was alone which was good as I was planning on going home without them knowing I had left. I still did not fully trust the Mystical Knights, I still felt like they were hiding something from me and what if my dream was true, maybe the Mystical Knights also wanted to use the jewel for themselves.

I had a look at the bikes and my plan to escape back home vanished, mine had scratches down one side and a flat tire, Nick's bike had the same damage but with an added dent to the handlebars. I could not fix them. Looks like I will be walking home, I noticed an old knife next to some tools beside the bikes so I picked it up, it wasn't very sharp and had rust around the handle, but it would have to do, so I put it in my belt. I sighed out loud at the thought of walking home, but I know Dark Forest like the back of my hand, I know ways through it others don't, I will get back to Unicorn Stables. Everyone there must be worried.

I slowly crept out of the shed and looked around; no one was there so I quickly walked through the gate that led back to the forest. Once I was further up the track I glanced behind me, but no one was in sight, good I don't think I've been spotted I thought. I got closer to the forest but stopped as I had second thoughts about going alone and I suddenly heard a noise behind me, the sound of a horse trotting towards me, oh no, I have been caught.

I turned around and saw a lovely black horse coming towards me and sitting on the horse was an angry Tristan. He stopped his horse in front of me and shouted, "Are you planning on walking home!"

"Yes." I said.

"After everything that just happened and everything we have told you, do you think that's a clever idea." He snarled.

"I........." Ok so he does have a good point, but I am not going to hide behind a group of people I hardly know or trust.

"I can take care of myself." I said quietly.

"You mean like you did last time, this isn't a joke, this is serious you could get killed!" He yelled.

"I'm not stupid! I know that. Nick got hurt because of me, I didn't ask for this jewel, I didn't want this to happen I'm scared, and I don't know what to do but I will not let fear control me, next time I will be ready. If you want to be the hero then you're welcome to tag along." I shouted back.

Tristan's horse backed up startled. I felt angry so I stormed off and entered the forest, I was still going home whether he liked it or not.

I suddenly felt weak and had to sit down on a nearby log to catch my breath, so much for looking like I can handle myself, I thought. Tristan pulled his horse up to stop beside me.

"Are you tired already?" He smiled.

"I'm just having a little rest, if I'm going too slow for you then just go away." I snapped.

"Rose I'm not going anywhere, Isabella explained to me you used up half of your energy using your magic, so stop being stubborn and get on the back of my horse." I looked back up at him and saw that he had his hand held out to me and he was smiling.

"Come on you know you want to; it will be quicker getting home." he said.

"Are you really going to take me back home?" I asked.

"Yes, if that's what you want." He replied.

I took a deep breath he was right, I got to my feet and Tristan's horse turned his head towards me and neighed at me in greeting. I laughed and stroked his white stripe on his face, "Ok you win, what's his name?"

"Patrick and he can be stubborn too." Tristan replied with a smile.

I smiled back and took his hand, and he pulled me up behind him as though I weighed as much as a

feather, so that is the strength of a shapeshifter, I thought.
I held onto his back, he told Patrick to go, and we took off back through the Dark Forest.

Chapter 7.
Surprises from the enemy.

Tristan was right, it was faster; in fact, it was a lot faster than before when we had journeyed to Old House as the path was a lot clearer, so it was easier to get through. Once we arrived in front of the stables we dismounted off Patrick and walked through the gate, Silver popped his head out of his stable and neighed, so I gave him a pat on his nose.
"Hello boy, did you miss me?" Silver nodded his head and neighed again, Tristan and I both laughed. Patrick got closer to Silver's stable, and Tristan introduced him, they both became friends straight away. Well maybe I could trust Tristan, Silver seemed to like him and Patrick, so maybe I should try.

I told Tristan he could put Patrick in a spare stable near Silver's, so he could come into the house to get a drink and have a rest. We got to the front door of the house but before I could go inside Tristan pushed me to the floor, I looked up to yell at him, but he was also on the ground, and I found myself face to face with a shadow demon. It gave me a creepy smile which was black and hollow, fear welled up inside of me, before Tristan could get up to fight it dropped something beside me then fled to the forest.
Tristan was beside me in seconds "Are you alright?" He asked with concern.
"I'm fine, but a little warning next time." I said as I picked up the letter the shadow had dropped.
"Sorry, what does it say?" He asked as he helped pull me back up to my feet.
I unfolded the paper and inside was a message written in red ink, my blood ran cold as I read it out

loud. "I hope you like your surprise, love from Finn."
We both looked at each other then ran inside the
house; we heard pots and pans banging in the
kitchen, so we headed there first. I quickly pushed
open the door. A glass smashed to the floor and
everyone who was sat eating at the table jumped to
their feet in surprise.
I looked around the room and noticed that everyone
who lived at Unicorn Stables was in this room, even
Spencer who barked at us as we entered. I took a
deep breath; I was glad everyone looked alright.
"Rose!" Shouted Hannah and she ran to me to give
me a hug.
"Is everyone alright?" I asked as I hugged her back.
"We were going to ask you that, maybe warn us next
time by knocking on the door so we know you are
there and walk in, you scared the hell out of us." Said
Anthony as he walked over to Helen to help her clean
up the glass she dropped.
"Sorry, but......" I looked at Tristan; he shrugged his
shoulders at me, great he was not very helpful I
thought.
"What's wrong dear? Why don't you both come and
sit down you both look exhausted." Said Willow with
concern.
"Well, we should really go and check the rest of the
house first, right Tristan?" I said.
He nodded "I will go and look outside; I suggest the
rest of you should go in groups to check the other
rooms in the house, if anyone sees anything that
shouldn't be there shout me." He left the room.
The others looked at me confused "What the hell is
that magic user talking about?" Shouted James, he
looked mad.
"Well, something called a shadow demon ran out of
the house when we arrived so we were worried you

were in danger, I think we should check the rest of the house like Tristan said to make sure there aren't any more." I explained a little too quickly.

"What!" Shouted Helen.

"A shadow demon in our house!" Shouted Jack.

"I knew these magic users would bring nothing but trouble." Said James angrily.

"Oh no!" cried Hannah, then she ran to Willow.

"Everyone calm down, we will do what Rose said. Anthony, Jack, and James you three check the rooms downstairs, Helen and Rose can check upstairs I will wait here with Hannah and Spencer, if anyone sees anything weird or out of place call for Tristan he seems to know what he's doing but please be careful there could be more of those shadows about." Said Willow with a calm but firm voice.

"Alright guys you heard her lets go." Said Anthony who took the lead and left the room, the rest of us followed and split up in our groups.

Helen and I headed upstairs, I went first, if something were to jump out at us it would be better if I got hurt and not her, as I knew deep down this was all my fault, I had put the others in danger. We searched all the rooms in silence listening out for anything unusual; we were both on high alert. We looked under all the beds searched through all the cupboards and peeked behind the curtains. There are nine rooms upstairs, the bathroom and four bedrooms were on the second floor and the last four bedrooms were up another set of stairs on the third floor, all the rooms looked the same and nothing jumped out at us, but as we got to the last room which was my room on the third floor when I opened the door I noticed something different, something strange.

I pointed to the desk and Helen looked, on top was a

single red rose in a glass vase. We both looked at each other then slowly moved towards the desk; Helen gasped
"Is that blood?"
I looked closer at the rose petals a red liquid was dripping from them and instead of water in the vase, it was the same red liquid, and it did look like blood.
I took a deep breath and reached out for the card that I had noticed near the vase I opened it to read the message inside,
`Dear Rose, we are going to have so much fun together I just hope none of your friends get in my way again, love Finn.'

I looked up at Helen who had read the note over my shoulder, her face was pale with fear then she suddenly ran out of the room and yelled.
"Tristan!"
I could hear her running down the corridor then back down the stairs to look for him. I froze, I felt sick I did not know what to do, what did the note mean and whose blood was that? I was thinking all this, as I heard footsteps running towards my room. I turned around, Tristan ran in followed by Anthony, Helen, Jack, and James.
Tristan looked at me, then at the vase on the desk; he walked towards it to have a closer look.
"Damn, is that blood?" Asked Anthony.
"Yes and don't worry it's just Finn's blood he's doing this to scare you." Said Tristan who looked back at me.
"That boy who attacked you in the forest?" Asked Jack, Helen nodded.
"And how the hell do you know it's Finn's blood?" Shouted James who still didn't trust Tristan.

"I'm a shapeshifter, I can smell it." Explained Tristan. The room went quiet as everyone took in what he had just said; I forgot they didn't know about him. I read the note again, maybe I have missed something, is there a hidden message in this? I thought. Jack had noticed me reading so he looked over my shoulder and read the note out loud for the others to hear.

"So, he's threatening us now." Said Anthony with anger.

"This is why I hate magic users." Said James.

"Rose, are you alright?" Asked Helen, she had noticed me clench my fists. Before I could reply Tristan growled picked up the vase and then snatched the note from my hand and left the room muttering "I need to make a call."

"OK, now that the shapeshifter has left the room, what should we do?" Asked Anthony.

"I can't believe it; can we even trust him, who is he calling and how?" Said James with a confused look.

"Maybe he has one of those S.C.D. we've heard some magic users carry, if the stories are true." Said Anthony.

S.C.D. stands for Stone Communication Device, they can only be used by magic users to send messages by talking through the device to each other, and they somehow power it with their magic. My mother told me the fairies made them and it is faster to send messages using it instead of writing letters like we have to.

I shrugged and said, "I…I think we can trust him; he did save me and Nick." I could tell the others still weren't happy.

"I'm going to tell Willow what's happened; maybe she will know what to do." Said Helen and she left the room, the others started to follow her out, but I stayed behind.

Jack had noticed, "Aren't you coming Rose." He asked.

"I will come soon, but I want to check the rest of my room first." I replied.

He nodded then left with the others and I quickly shut the door behind him, I could feel the jewel heating up around my neck and it had started to glow again but this time it was a shade of blue, I wonder if it's because I feel worried and confused. I took a deep breath to calm down and the jewel became cooler. I then investigated the rest of my room but there were no other surprises and nothing else was out of place, so I sat down on the edge of my bed to rest. I still felt tired, and my bruises and cuts felt sore.

After a while there was a sudden knock on my door that made me jump.

"Rose dear, it's me can I come in?" Shouted Willow.

I took another deep breath, "Yes."

She opened the door then came to sit beside me, "Are you alright dear?" She asked with concern.

I nodded and replied, "Yes I'm fine."

She could tell I was lying so she gave me a hug, "My brave girl don't worry I am sure everything will work out fine in the end, you are one of the strongest girls I know so I know you can handle magic. The others have just checked the horses and everything outside is ok but I am going to let Tristan stay here in the spare room tonight so he can keep an eye on us, if that's alright with you?"

I wiped my eyes and answered, "OK."

"Good, now why don't we go and get something to eat with the others, that should make you feel better." She said as she left the room, I nodded and followed her back down the stairs.

We both walked back into the dining room, and everyone looked happy to see us but also worried. They were all sat at the table eating except for Tristan he was stood near the window looking out. Willow and I sat down at the table with the others, our plates were already filled with chicken and rice, and it looked and smelled lovely.

The room was quiet while we ate which was unusual because normally we would be telling each other stories and laughing together. I could tell the others were not happy about Tristan staying, he had just admitted he was a shapeshifter after all. I could see them glancing at him and whispering things to each other and I knew for a fact Tristan could hear every word. I picked up his cup of tea that was still on the table and walked over to him to talk.

I passed him the cup and said, "Here, don't let it get cold."

"Thanks." He smiled then took a sip.

"So, is everything alright outside, there aren't any more shadows?" I asked as I looked out the window, the sky looked darker.

"Everything looked normal out there and I checked the horses with the others while we fed them, and they seem fine. I don't think there are any more shadows about, but Odin told me to stay and keep an eye on everyone and keep you safe." He said and touched a device attached to his belt, so he did have an S.C.D.

He swallowed some more tea out of his cup, and I looked again out of the window the clouds were gathering in the sky, a storm was coming.

Tristan snarled, "Don't worry nothing is going to get passed me."

I smiled, "Thanks for helping us."

"That's my job." He replied.

"Well, you should get something to eat; there is a plate on the table for you, I'm sure panthers like chicken."

He laughed, "Yes, thank you chicken will be fine."

We both sat back down at the table and Tristan dug into his food, but I couldn't finish mine I wasn't very hungry, and I just kept thinking about the note Finn left and everything else that had happened. Helen had noticed my plate was not empty as she collected the plates to wash,

"Are you feeling alright Rose?" She asked.

"Um…Yeah thanks for dinner, I'm just not that hungry." I told her.

I noticed the others looking at me so I smiled and left the table, I decided to sit on the window seat so I could watch the storm.

The clouds looked worse, and it had started to rain, a large boom of thunder made me jump and suddenly the lights went out. Spencer barked and Hannah screamed, she has never liked thunder.

"Don't worry, the storm has just knocked the light stones out, it's happened before." Said Willow as she tried to calm her down.

Light stones power the lights and oven in the house by storing the light from the sun and moon inside, but sometimes when storms come it can knock the light out of them and everything powered by them will turn off. These and the seer stones in the stone lens's that are used to take photos and record are the only things magic related in this house. The fairies found these stones long ago and now sell them at markets to help everyone, though some people would rather not use them, and still use fire for light and to cook instead.

"Ouch, you've just stood on my foot James." Shouted Jack.

The Magical Jewel, A Mystical Knight Novel, Book 1.
By Jade Stephenson ©.

The jewel around my neck suddenly lit up a bright white to light the room. I started to panic; how do I stop this I thought, but then a hand touched my shoulder it was Tristan.

"Don't worry it's just giving us some light so we can see again." I looked at the others they were staring at me with shock and fear in their eyes. I took a deep breath to calm down and the jewel dulled down a little.

"Well, that's helpful. Anthony could you please light the fire." Said Willow.

Anthony nodded and started to light the fire and Helen threw some more wood on it, the jewel faded back down to purple as the fire burned to light the room instead. Everyone sat down in the other chairs in front of the fire, except Tristan he sat beside me near the window and watched the storm with me. Another boom of thunder sounded outside; we sat in silence as we listened. More thunder and a crack of lightning flashed but then another noise was heard outside. Drumming!

I jumped to my feet, I had heard that noise before and so had Tristan, his eyes lit up a brighter green as he looked out of the window.

"What on earth is that noise?" Said Helen who had also jumped up. The others ran to the windows to join us to see if we could see anything, but it was too dark. Spencer started to growl and then we heard more noises, it sounded like people screaming and wolves howling.

"What the hell is going on out there?" Yelled James.

"I don't like this!" Cried Hannah who was still hugging Willow.

"It's alright, we should be safe in here." She did not sound too convincing as she sat back down in one of the chairs with a sigh.

The noises became louder as though they were

closing in on the house and as more lightning flashed I spotted something outside.

"Did you see that?" I shouted.

They all looked at me, "No, what was it?" Asked Anthony.

"I didn't see it clearly but I...I think it looked like a wolf, but I only saw its shadow." I explained. Everyone looked back out the window and we heard another terrified scream.

"I think I should go outside to look; someone might be hurt." Said Anthony but Helen put her hand out and grabbed his arm to stop him.

"Are you crazy?"

"He's right, I will go with you. We should also check the horses." I said and turned to leave.

"NO!" Yelled Tristan with anger.

We all turned to look at him and noticed he was holding a dagger; he must have had it tucked away in his belt. We all took a step back from him which I could tell annoyed him, but I could also see sadness in his eyes he knew we did not trust him.

I moved back towards him and asked, "What's wrong?"

"No one is leaving this house." He said.

"What do you mean?" Shouted James with a scared look.

"But...." I started to complain but he interrupted.

"Take this." He held out the dagger and I took it.

"Now, I'm going outside to check things out, the rest of you stay here." he said, then he walked towards the door.

"Wait you can't go by yourself it might be dangerous." I said.

He looked back at me and smiled, "Don't worry about me; I'll be fine just stay here with the others." Then he left the room, we heard the front door open then close behind him and Anthony went to lock the door behind him.

We all ran back to the windows to see if we could see Tristan, but we couldn't, we heard more howls and then the drumming stopped. It became silent, the only noise now was the fire crackling and the rain outside, even the thunder had stopped for now. We waited but there was still no sign of Tristan.

"Maybe one of us should have gone with him." I said. The others stayed quiet and kept watch out the window.

Then we suddenly heard knocking on the front door, Spencer barked again and ran to the door, but Hannah pulled him away so the rest of us could run out the kitchen to investigate.

"Be careful." Shouted Willow who had stayed behind with Hannah and Spencer.

We got to the front door then stopped, the glow of the fire from the kitchen was helping but it was still a lot darker in the corridor. The jewel helped by lighting up again. We could still hear the knocking, but it didn't sound right and there was a scratching noise too.

"So should we open it?" Asked Jack.

"I don't think so, it could be anything." Said Anthony.

"We have to, what if Tristan needs our help." I said then walked to the door with the dagger in my hand pointing forward.

"No Rose, let me go first." Said Anthony and he took the dagger from me.

I nodded, he reached out and opened the door a little to peep out. Then he quickly slammed it shut again.

"What is it Anthony?" Asked Helen with a tremble in her voice.

He looked shocked and scared, "It's crazy but there is a panther out there, a huge black panther." He whispered and moved away from the door.

I took a deep breath then reached out to open the door.

"Rose! What are you doing?" Asked Helen.

"I'm letting him in." I replied.

"What!" Everyone shouted and Anthony tried to pull me away, but it was too late, I opened the door and the panther walked in.

The others backed away and Anthony pointed the dagger at him.

"Rose, what have you done?" Yelled Helen.

I stepped in front of Anthony and put myself in between the dagger and Tristan.

"Don't worry it's just Tristan, remember he's a shapeshifter." I explained.

"You're kidding, right?" Asked James with fear.

"No, I'm not; this is Tristan, so Anthony please put the dagger down."

Anthony looked down and noticed the dagger was pointing at my heart, so he quickly lowered it, but he kept his eyes on Tristan.

"Wait, how do you know it's Tristan? It could be another panther." Said Jack.

I turned around and looked at the panther, I had not thought of that, but somehow just by looking at him I had known it was Tristan.

"It is him." I said.

"Damn it Rose, next time warn us before you open the door." Yelled Helen.

And that's when I remembered I hadn't told everyone what Tristan could change into. "I'm sorry, I…"

"I'm sick of all this weird magic and anyone that can use magic shouldn't be allowed in this house." Helen yelled then ran upstairs, rather well considering the lights were still off. Jack and James followed her up at a slower pace except for Anthony who handed me back the dagger and said,

"I'm going to tell Willow we're fine." Then he walked back to the kitchen.

I sighed out loud then looked back towards the door, maybe I should leave I've brought nothing but trouble, I thought.

Tristan sat in front of the door and looked at me with his big green eyes; it's like he somehow knew what I was thinking.

"Maybe next time you should change back into a human before coming into the house." I said to him, but he just shook his head, he must not be able to change back yet for some reason.

"So, is everything alright outside now? Did you see anything?" I asked.

He bowed his head, and I wondered if that was a yes to both questions, this is going to be a difficult night, trying to communicate with a panther is hard work, I thought as I watched him lick his leg clean. And that's when I saw the blood; he had been injured, so there had been something out there after all.

I walked up to him and knelt down beside him to have a closer look,

"It doesn't look too deep I think you should be fine." I said and I held my hand out to touch his leg and make sure he wasn't hurt somewhere else, but Tristan moved out of the way and snarled at me.

"There is no need to snarl at me, I was only seeing if you were alright." I snapped then ran off up the stairs to my bedroom before I got too angry. This was going to be a long night, I thought as I slammed my door shut behind me.

Chapter 8.
Magic Training.

I was surrounded by darkness; it was cold, and I could hear the drumming. Hundreds of shadow demons appeared all around me, and the strange boy wrapped in a black cloak walked up to me, I still could not see his face.

"I'm coming to rescue you Rose, I am coming to take you away, and you will join the Shadow guild and understand it's for the best." He said.

The shadows started laughing which hurt my head; I covered my ears with my hands and cried "No!"

Then another boy appeared next to me, I had seen him before but in a photograph. He had long black hair and a short beard and he looked strong, but what stood out the most were his bright green eyes.

"Stay away from her." He growled.

The other boy took a step back and he looked shocked.

"You! How is this possible, you should be dead." He then pointed his hand towards us, and the shadows lunged forward to attack. I screamed and the boy with the green eyes yelled,

"Rose wake up!" I heard a roar; I screamed again then I woke up.

I quickly sat up in bed I was out of breath and scared, the jewel that I had left around my neck last night was sparkling a dark blue and was crackling like lighting around me and my room, I could not make it stop. My bedroom door flew open, and Tristan ran in.

"Rose are you alright? What happened?" He yelled with concern.

"I…. I don't know, I had a bad dream and when I woke

69

up the jewel was like this, and it won't stop." I cried.
The jewel heated up and more sparks flew out around
my room. Helen and Anthony were suddenly at the
door, but they were too scared to enter.
"What's going on?" Shouted Helen.
"Stay back!" Yelled Tristan, then he sat beside me on
the bed and took hold of my hand.
"Listen Rose, your jewel is connected to your
emotions, it reacts to your feelings it must have felt
your fear, you need to think of something that will
calm you down, the nightmare is over now, take a
deep breath and close your eyes, you can do it."
I looked into his bright green eyes and nodded, I
closed my eyes and took a deep breath, I tried to
think of something that would help calm me down, but
I kept seeing the shadows attacking and the strange
boy wrapped in darkness.
I heard the voice in my head again, "**You can do it
Rose, listen to my brother**."
I took another deep breath then heard Helen shout,
"Rose, think of animals you are always calm around
them, think of Silver."
I smiled she was right, no matter how bad I felt being
around animals and riding Silver always made me feel
better. It helped, I felt calmer and the jewel around my
neck started to cool down. I opened my eyes and
Tristan smiled at me,
"See I knew you could control it; you will be alright
now." He said.
"Thank you." I said.
He nodded let go of my hand then got up and left the
room.
Helen and Anthony stayed behind but I noticed they
still would not come into my room, then I noticed Jack,
James and Hannah peeping around them. I wondered
how long they had been there.

"Is Rose alright now?" Asked Hannah.
Helen turned around "Yes she's fine, lets leave so she can get dressed and we can have some breakfast."
"Thank you Helen." I said, she smiled and shut the door behind her as she followed the others downstairs.
I noticed everyone looked as tired as I was, we could hardly sleep last night because we kept hearing more noises and the howling, the thunder had also continued throughout the night so that didn't help. I thought back to the events that happened in the night:

'I had climbed out of bed to go and check on the others and noticed they had all paired up to sleep in the same rooms, even Spencer had decided to sleep in Helen's room with Hannah. I was not sure if it was because of the noises or because a large black panther was walking around our house. I had gone downstairs to get a glass of water and to make sure it was still safe, when I had noticed Tristan back in human form sat in the kitchen with a glass of milk. Well, I nearly laughed out loud he really was just a big pussy cat, but I stayed quiet as I didn't want to offend him or get him mad again. He had smiled at me and apologized for snarling at me, then he had asked if I was alright. I lied and told him I was fine, then took my water straight back upstairs to bed, as I was still mad, not at him but at the whole situation I was in.'

I sighed out loud and decided to stop thinking about last night and get out of bed. I opened my curtains and noticed the storm had cleared and the sun felt warm, after a quick shower I threw on a tee-shirt and a pair of shorts then headed downstairs. I didn't go into the kitchen where I knew the others were; I left the house and walked to Silver's stable.

The Magical Jewel, A Mystical Knight Novel, Book 1.
By Jade Stephenson ©.

All the horses had already been mucked out and fed
and a few had even been turned out into the fields. I
decided to groom Silver and tack him up for a ride
out, most days I didn't need to put any tack on Silver
to ride him, as he lets me ride him without it and he
always seems to know where I need to go, but
sometimes if I plan on going on longer rides or take
him to the village I use his tack. I also decided to put
on some saddle bags to pack some extra things I may
need.
As I finished putting on the saddle bags I heard
someone approach the stable, I turned and saw
Willow walk in.
"Morning dear, how are you feeling?" She asked.
"Morning, I feel a little better now but still tired, I'm
hoping a ride out will wake me up. I'm going to Old
House to find out more about this jewel."
"Good, yes that's a good idea I'm sure Robert and the
others will explain everything to you, I think Tristan
has just gone to tack his horse up, so please don't
leave without him."
"I won't, I have to go and pack my bag first." I said
without thinking.
"Pack a bag, what do you mean?" She asked with
concern.
"Sorry I forgot I didn't tell you; I was thinking maybe I
should stay at Old House for a while if they will let me.
I think it would be for the best while I learn how to
control the magic in this jewel and so you and the
others won't be in any more danger. If that's alright
with you." I told her.
Willow took hold of my hands and said, "My darling
girl if that's what you want then I won't stop you, I'm
sure Robert and everyone there will be happy to have
you, but please remember myself and everyone here
at Unicorn Stables will always help and support you

no matter what happens, so if you need to come back home you are always welcome here, you are a part of our family after all."

I smiled and nodded "Thank you Willow."

We both left Silver's stable and walked back towards the house, but Willow stopped as I opened the door. "I'm going to go talk with Tristan while you pack your bag, and please make sure you take some food with you, it will give you energy." She said and walked off to find Tristan.

Once I was back in my room I changed into some jodhpurs and started to pack some clothes into a bag and some other things I may need, then I went back downstairs and into the kitchen to grab some food and a bottle of water to take with me.

As I was eating an apple and wondering if I should take anything else Helen, Anthony, Jack, James, and Hannah walked in, they must have been outside with the horses. James was the first one to speak,

"So, is it true, are you really going to live with the magic users?" He asked me.

I took another bite of my apple, swallowed, and nodded.

"Are you crazy?" Shouted Jack.

"I don't have a choice I have to, it's the only way I am going to learn how to control this jewel so it will be safe, and I don't want to put any of you in more danger." I said.

"Don't be stupid Rose; you're the one who will be in danger if you live with them!" Yelled Helen.

"If I don't learn how to control the magic inside this jewel someone will get hurt and if I don't leave, the shadows might come back and hurt one of you, so like I said before I don't have a choice." I shouted back and threw the last bit of apple in the bin.

"We understand Rose, but...." Before Anthony could

finish he was interrupted.

"No, we don't, we don't even know them, and how do you know we can trust them? For all we know these magic users could be the evil ones trying to take Rose away from us!" Yelled James.

"That's enough everyone." Willow said.

We all turned around to face her, she had entered the kitchen with Tristan behind her and I could tell by the look on his face he had heard everything we had just said, he did not look pleased. Willow continued,

"If Rose wants to go we should not stop her, it's her decision to make. I trust Robert and I am sure Rose trusts Tristan and that's why she has chosen to go. If you lot don't trust the magic users that's your choice, but you should at least trust Rose you have all known her long enough."

Everyone fell silent as they thought about what Willow had just said, and then Hannah ran up to me and gave me a hug.

"I trust you Rose but come home soon, ok."

I hugged her back, "Thanks, you don't have to worry about me I will be back in no time, you'll see." I looked up at the others and they all nodded.

"I'm ready to leave when you are." Said Tristan who was still stood at the door.

"Alright, lets go." I replied and followed him out of the room.

Once we got back to the stables we both mounted our horses and headed off up the track towards the forest. I turned around to have another look at Unicorn Stables and hoped I was making the right choice, and that's when I saw everyone standing at the gate waving at me to say goodbye. I smiled and waved back then I urged Silver on into a trot then a canter, before I changed my mind and stayed. I could hear Tristan and Patrick following.

The Magical Jewel, A Mystical Knight Novel, Book 1.
By Jade Stephenson ©.

The ride through the forest had luckily been uneventful but I could tell Tristan had been on high alert as he had expected trouble. At every sound we both seemed to jump and stop until we knew what had made the noise, it was normally some forest creature moving about. Once we arrived at Old House we un-tacked our horses and put them both in one of the fields together, as Silver and Patrick were getting on fine we decided to head into the house to see Odin. We found him in his office sitting at his desk and writing. He looked up as we both entered and smiled,

"Ah, hello. I'm glad to see you both made it back here safe and sound, I hope the journey wasn't too rough for you." He said.

"Everything is alright, nothing happened on the way here." Replied Tristan.

"Good, I am sorry to hear about last night, Tristan filled me in on the details I hope you and your family weren't too frightened. Don't worry we will make sure you, and the others stay safe." Said Odin and I could tell he meant what he said.

"Thank you." I said.

Odin nodded and said, "Tristan informs me you would also like to stay here with us, is that true?"

"Yes, I believe everyone at Unicorn Stables is struggling with magic appearing around their home, you see a few of them have had bad experiences with magic users. So I don't want to cause them any more problems, I need to learn how to control this jewel, so no one is in danger because of me. I thought staying here would be the best choice, if that is alright with you?" I asked him.

"I see, of course staying here is definitely the best choice, in fact I was going to suggest it myself, but I was worried asking you to leave your home would be too much to ask of you considering what you are going through, but we would be happy to have you here and we will do all we can to help you." Said Odin.

"Of course we will, you have a good heart Rose, so I know teaching you magic won't be a problem." Said Isabella who had just walked into the office behind us, smiling.

"Good, it's settled then. Rose will be staying here now, Tristan if you could go and tell the others and ask Marigold and Clover to get a room ready for her. Rose you can leave your bag here, myself and Isabella will start teaching you straight away, we will go outside." Said Odin who stood up, picked up his sword and followed us out of the room.

After we had left the office, I found myself standing in the garden beside Old House with Odin and Isabella, Tristan had gone off to find the other magic users. Around us wooden targets were set up and there were bows and arrows in a basket near us. I looked around wondering how this was meant to help me with magic training. Isabella picked up a bow and handed it to me then she got one for herself, she took an arrow out of the basket in front of us then pointed at the basket. I understood what she wanted me to do so I also picked up an arrow.

"So, I guess you're wondering what this has got to do with magic training." She said, I nodded.

"Well, we are going to teach you some attacks that you can use to defend yourself from shadows or anyone else if you need to, but first you need to learn how to aim, have you ever shot an arrow before?" She asked.

"Well, me and Nick had toy bows when we were kids,

but I don't think that counts." I smiled and
remembered I was better at shooting the arrows than
Nick which used to get him mad.
Isabella laughed and said, "Well the aiming technique
is the same, but you are right this will be harder to get
used to, here I will show you first." She took a deep
breath, pulled back the arrow then released it. The
arrow soared through the air and hit the middle of one
of the targets with a bang.
"Wow! your good." I said.
"Thank you; I have had a lot of practice." She replied.
"That's right, she's a champion at Sunlight City, you
see you don't have to use magic to be a part of the
Mystical Knights." Explained Odin who had been
watching.
"Really! So, you can't use magic?" I asked her.
"No, but you still need to know a lot about magic to be
a knight, I also chose to learn how to fight, to be of
more help to the knights and so I can help protect my
family and friends." Explained Isabella.
"After seeing Tristan was a shapeshifter I was trying
to guess what the rest of you could do, I thought
maybe you were a fairy like Marigold and Clover but
with a different eye color." I said.
"So, you have figured it out already, we were going to
tell you, but we didn't want to scare you, we know
how some people fear and hate them, so we weren't
sure how to tell you." Said Odin.
"With flower names and gold eyes it's not hard to
figure it out, and my mother used to tell me good
stories about fairies and shapeshifters, so you don't
have to worry I don't hate them, and I understand why
you didn't tell me, some of the villagers around here
aren't keen on magic users." I explained.
"Well, your mother must have been a special lady."
Said Odin.

I smiled, "Yeah she was."

"Well, I think it's your turn to try Rose, you can shoot at a closer target, that one there, remember to keep both eyes open and concentrate as best as you can, then let the arrow fly." said Isabella who pointed at a closer target in front of us, I nodded.

I stood how Isabella had and nocked my arrow to the bow string, then I took a deep breath pulled back the arrow and released it. I managed to hit the target, but it wasn't in the middle it was near the bottom.

"Excellent Rose with a bit more practice you should hit the middle in no time." Said Odin.

"He's right Rose normally beginners don't hit the target straight away, you're a natural." Said Isabella who smiled at me.

"Um.....Thanks." I said as I rubbed my eyes.

"Is something wrong?" Asked Odin.

"Yeah, does the jewel affect your sight? Because while I was aiming my eyes started to focus better, well it was more like my eyes were trying to zoom in on the target." I replied and rubbed my eyes again, it had felt weird.

Odin and Isabella both looked at each other with shock.

"What, is that bad?" I asked nervously.

"No, I don't think so, it's just that we have never heard the jewel doing that before, in fact only shapeshifters have that ability." Said Odin.

"So, what does that mean? I won't turn into an animal, will I?" I asked with concern.

"No, it's nothing like that, you have to be born with the ability to do that, but maybe the jewel has more powers than we originally thought. I wouldn't worry about it though, I'm sure you will get used to it in time, have you noticed anything else different about yourself?" Said Odin.

"Well, my hearing has been quite good since I can remember but lately it feels different, I think it has improved too, I can hear things further away and more clearly." I explained.

"Well, that should be good for you but if anything else happens please tell us so we can try to help you the best we can. I think training with Tristan should help you get used to your sight and hearing." He said but he still looked puzzled.

"Why don't you try hitting another target Rose, see if you can hit the middle this time, try to relax but concentrate on the middle of the target and see if that will help your eyes adjust." Said Isabella.

"Right."

I did the same and my eyes started to zoom in on the target again, but I didn't let it put me off this time I took another deep breath and let the arrow fly as the middle of the target came into focus, I heard a bang as I hit my target.

"Well done Rose, you did it." Said Isabella with a smile.

"Yes but it is going to take me a while to get used to my eyes zooming in and out, it feels weird." I said and rubbed my eyes again.

"I'm sure you will manage Rose, now I think you're ready to use magic." Said Odin.

"What!"

"Don't worry I know you can do it; you have already done it in the forest. Now let me show you first how I use my weapon." Odin said and pulled out his sword from its sheath.

It was a long-bladed sword with a thick wooden hilt, it looked like a normal sword but when I looked closer I could see different colored jewels on the pommel and weird symbols around the grip.

"Now, it may look like a normal knightly sword or

spatha, but it is not, this sword is a rare magical item and it's named Zeus. You saw me use it in the forest when we helped you, I will show you how I use it."
Odin stood next to us in a stance that looked like he was about to stab someone, he aimed with his sword at a target and thrust forward, a bright yellow light shot from the sword and hit the target in the middle, a black burn mark appeared on the spot.
"Wow, remind me not to get into a fight with you." I said in awe.
Odin and Isabella laughed "Yes, it is a powerful weapon, and it can be used with or without magic, to make it fire lightning bolts I simply think about it, picture it is happening in my mind. You can also do this with your jewel, but you can use any weapon as long as you wear the jewel, I can only use this sword." He said.
I nodded as I took all this in; I think I understood what he was saying.
Before he could continue the lesson suddenly a ball of fire shot passed my head and hit one of the targets, it burst into flames.
"Edmund! You idiot!" Shouted Isabella.
I turned around and saw Edmund smirking at me; Tristan, Marigold and Clover were beside him.
Odin sighed, "Marigold, could you?" he said and pointed at the target on fire.
Marigold nodded and lifted her hand in the air; water shot out of her hand flew through the air and hit the target putting the flames out.
"Cool! I didn't know fairies could do that." I said and smiled at Marigold.
She blushed and said, "So they have told you what we are."
"We didn't need to she had already worked it out, Rose is a smart girl." Said Odin.

"My mother told me great stories about fairies and shapeshifters." I explained to the others.

Odin nodded and explained, "All fairies have some ability to control the elements, but Marigold's water magic mainly comes from her magical item, the bracelet Aquarius." He pointed to the blue bracelet around Marigold's wrist.

"Wow." I said as I looked at the shiny bracelet with blue stones.

"Hey, why isn't anyone impressed with my magic." Moaned Edmund and he pointed to his red ring on his finger, so that must be how he controls fire.

"Well maybe it's because their magic is better." Laughed Clover.

"What! That's not funny." Replied Edmund and he started to chase Clover around the garden, the others laughed. I could tell they all cared deeply for each other; they weren't all related by blood, but it didn't matter they were a family just like mine.

Maybe I could trust them, but deep down I still felt as though they were hiding something from me, before I could think about what it was, Odin spoke.

"Now Rose why don't you try hitting the target again, but this time do what I did, picture lightning firing from the arrow too. Take a deep breath and clear your mind and imagine your energy is moving through your body to the bow then the arrow and pull back and fire."

I nodded took another deep breath and did what he said, my eyes still zoomed in on the target which did not help my concentration so when I fired no magic appeared but on the second attempt the arrow hit the middle of the target but this time there was a small light on the tip of the arrow. Odin walked up to the target to have a closer look then he said,

"Well done Rose with more practice you should be

able to make the magic stronger in no time."
I nodded but I was worried I didn't want stronger
magic I just wanted it to stay under control, so I didn't
hurt anyone.

The magic users decided to let me keep practicing
alone but they stayed close in case I needed them.
Isabella was the closest as she had decided to
practice with her own bow, Odin and Tristan were
sword fighting, Edmund was taking a nap in the sun
while Marigold was making some new curtains for the
house and Clover was sat near them both drawing
pictures.
Every time I fired the arrow the magic did look
stronger, and I was starting to get used to my eyes
adjusting while I aimed which helped me hit the other
targets that were further away.
However, there was still a fear in my mind that
stopped me from using too much magic and I kept
stopping to watch Tristan and Odin as their sword
fighting skills were amazing.
After another short break I started to fire another
arrow but as I did I suddenly spotted something dark
behind some bushes it reminded me of the shadow
demons and then I heard Finn laughing in my mind.
I flinched, then shot the arrow but to my surprise a
large purple flame flew through the air with it and hit
the target with a crash, the target blew up and the
other nearby targets caught fire. I fell to my knees
with fear, and I felt weak, what had happened? I
thought, but I already knew the answer, I had lost
control again.

Chapter 9.
Pain from the Past.

"Rose! Are you alright?" Shouted Isabella as she crouched beside me.

The other mystical knights ran up to us, I looked up and saw the garden on fire.

"I'm sorry.... I never.... I didn't mean to do that." I gasped.

Marigold raised her hands again and water appeared to extinguish the flames.

Odin knelt down beside me, "You are alright Rose, this can happen I should have noticed you were getting tired; I think we should stop your magic training for today, you have done well for your first practice."

"Yeah at least you hit the targets." Laughed Edmund.

I smiled but before I could reply we heard a yell from behind us.

"What on earth is going on here?" We all turned around; it was Claudia Brown the minister of the village.

Every village has a minister, they are in charge of most things that happen in the village, and they make sure all rules get followed correctly and if there is any trouble in their village concerning magic and the sheriff can't handle it then they can contact the king's knights from Sunlight City to deal with the problem. Claudia was a small woman in her late fifties, but she looked older, she loved to be in charge of everyone and everything, she also hated magic users. She wasn't alone, next to her was Agatha Mabel her assistant who was about the same age, wherever the minister went she would follow like a little lost lamb.

Also with them was Claudia's son Harry, a tall skinny boy who is a bully and likes to think he is in charge, he smirked at me, and I knew he wanted to start trouble.

"When I found out magic users were back living in my village and in this house I thought it was a lie, but no, here you are and by the looks of things you are already causing trouble." Said Claudia as she looked around at the burnt targets with disgust.

Odin stood and offered me his hand to help me up; once I was back on my feet he turned to face the visitors.

"Hello, can I help you with something, Miss?" He said.

"My name is Claudia Brown, and I am the minister of this village. I do not need help from you, but I would like you to stop using magic while you are here, as it's clearly dangerous." She replied and pointed at the burnt targets.

"I'm sorry..." I started to apologize, but Odin interrupted me,

"I am afraid we cannot do that; magic is a part of our lives so we will not stop and in the laws of our kingdom under section B3, no minister of any village is allowed to stop magic users from using magic unless they are causing trouble in which case the minister will contact the Mystical Knights who will then deal with the situation, also only the king has the authority to stop magic from being cast if needed."

The minister looked shocked, and I smiled, I don't think anyone has spoken to her like that before, most of the villagers were scared to in case she ordered them to leave the village. She finally noticed me standing there smiling.

"Rose, what are you doing here?" She said.

"Hello minister, I...." I looked around at the Mystical

Knights, no I was not going to lie, I wasn't going to let her bully me or the magic users so I said something I knew would shock them and make her mad.

"I'm just learning how to use magic with my new friends."

"Oh my!" Said Agatha.

"Now that's enough! Do you realize what day it is tomorrow? I will need you to be at your best." Said Claudia angrily.

I blinked, tomorrow? And then I remembered, the show jumping festival was tomorrow.

"Yes minister I will be there." I said which calmed her down.

"Good you better be, the whole village is counting on you, so I really don't think you should be messing around with magic." Claudia said then glanced at the magic users.

"I'm surprised you are here; your mother would be disappointed considering magic users caused her death." Said Harry with a grin.

"That was never proved true!" I shouted.

Claudia, Agatha, and Harry walked back up the track towards the carriage that was waiting for them to take them back to the village; I could hear Harry laughing as they left.

How dare he say that, how could he. I started to feel pain and anger in my heart.

"Rose?" Said Odin. The magic users were looking at the jewel with concern, I looked down and noticed it had turned pure black and smoke was coming out of it, and it also felt hot again. I took a deep breath and pictured Silver's face in my mind; the jewel slowly went back to normal.

"I'm fine, I need a drink." I said and headed back towards the house.

"Yes, me too I think we have some beer in the

kitchen." Smiled Edmund.

"Um…. I didn't mean that kind of drink."

"Just ignore him Rose, he's joking." Said Marigold then she hit him on the head.

"Ouch, how do you know?" He replied.

I smiled and headed back towards the house with the Mystical Knights, they kept glancing at the jewel, and I could tell they were worried; maybe it turning black like that was a bad sign.

We all sat around a table in the garden with our drinks to enjoy the warm sun. Isabella was the first one to speak,

"So, Rose what is happening in the village tomorrow?" She asked.

"Oh, sorry I forgot to tell you, it's the show jumping festival tomorrow other riders come from other villages nearby to compete to win the trophy, I will be the one to ride for our village again, there is also going to be stalls selling lots of food and gifts, it's a fun day for everyone." I explained.

"Good, I think we could all use a break; we should all go and cheer Rose on." Said Odin.

I smiled and took a sip from my drink, but the smile soon faded once he asked the next question,

"Now Rose I would like to ask you a personal question, one that I know upsets you, but it affected the jewel badly, so I think we need to know about it, what exactly did that boy mean when he said magic users were responsible for your mother's death?"

I took another sip from my drink before I answered, I could see the others were watching me closely to see if the jewel would react.

"It doesn't matter if you don't want to tell us Rose." Said Isabella.

I put my drink down on the table and said.

"No, it's alright someone else will probably tell you anyway so it's better if you hear the truth from me. My mother picked up an unknown illness which the doctors believed was caused by a poison only magic users can give you; the illness caused her to get weaker and weaker until she finally passed away. The doctors couldn't find any evidence that it was definitely magic users who caused her death but in the end a lot of people in the village believed that it was, though no matter how bad she got my mother kept saying magic was good, how could she say that, when all she felt was pain." Tears welled up in my eyes and the jewel turned dark again.

Odin got up from his chair and came over to my side, he knelt down beside me and took hold of both my hands and said.

"Your mother was a smart woman she must have known the villagers would think that and try to keep you away from magic users, but I think she wanted you to decide for yourself how to live your own life, Rose your life has been hard and it's only going to get harder, but I promise you, myself and the Mystical Knights will help protect you the best we can."

I smiled and wiped away my tears "Thank you."

Odin nodded and said, "It's alright."

"Hey, looks like we have another visitor." Said Edmund and pointed towards the track, we all looked up and spotted a horse running towards the house. I knew that horse, it was Murphy and Nick was riding him.

"It's Nick!" I shouted, got up from my chair and ran towards him.

Nick jumped down from Murphy as soon as he saw me and we both gave each other a hug, he then picked me up off the ground and swung me around in a circle, we both laughed out loud, we were happy to see each other.

He put me back down and said, "I'm glad you're safe Rose, are you alright?"

"I am now, how are you feeling?" I asked and looked at the bruise on his head, I had been worried about him since I last saw him being taken away from Old House, in fact I was going to go visit him later.

"Well, I'm a little sore but I'm more angry at myself for not protecting you better, big brothers are meant to protect their sisters, I'm sorry."

"Don't be stupid, you did protect me there is nothing else you could have done, we were up against magic. I guess I will have to fill you in on what happened." I said and smiled.

"No, it's alright, as soon as I woke up I insisted on going to see you, but my parents wanted me to eat first so by the time I got to Unicorn Stables, to my surprise you had moved out. Willow explained everything to me, though I still can't believe it." Nick said and looked at the jewel with concern.

The Mystical Knights walked up to us, and Odin spoke,

"Hello Nick, we are glad you are feeling well again, I'm sorry we didn't arrive sooner to help you."

"Hello, it's alright thank you for saving us and looking after Rose I know she can be trouble." Said Nick and laughed.

"Hey!" I laughed and hit him on the arm.

"Don't worry we will make sure you both stay safe in the future." Smiled Odin.

Nick nodded "I also have a message from Noah he's saying we need to start work on clearing the area where the stables are going and he also needs the plans, so I thought we could start now, if you're up to it." He looked at me again.

"Of course, that is our job, are you sure you're well

enough though?" I asked.

"Yeah, I'm fine but I can't stay long as I have to help my parents get the bakery ready for tomorrow." He replied.

"Alright, Clover and Marigold can show you the field where you can put your horse, the rest of us will help clear the area, it is where our horses will be living after all." Said Odin.

Once Nick, Marigold and Clover returned we all got to work picking up the broken bricks and wood, pulling out the weeds and sweeping up the mess. Tristan, Nick, and Odin also repaired some of the broken fence.

It was hard work and with every breath I took I was starting to feel weaker and weaker; it must be because I had used too much energy with magic practice.

I decided to sit down under one of the nearby trees to rest, Tristan must have noticed something was wrong as he came beside me and asked,

"Are you alright Rose?"

"Yes, I'm just having a break."

Odin knew I was lying, "Rose after you rest, why don't you start drawing the plans, the rest of us can finish this." He smiled.

"Ok." I smiled back.

After a while Nick said, "Well I better go now, my parents didn't want me staying long, you know how they worry, I will see you tomorrow Rose."

"Alright Nick, bye."

"Thank you for all your help." Said Odin.

"It's fine, bye." He waved at the others then went off to get Murphy ready to leave.

Once Nick had left, I went into Old House to get my

drawing pad and pencil so I could start drawing the plans for the stables, but I noticed my pencil was missing, I must have left it back at home. I went into Odin's office to borrow another one. He had unpacked more of his boxes and his desk was lined with old books and parchment, all his stuff looked and smelled old.

I went to his desk to find a pencil, but I spotted something that caught my eye, it was a large book that looked the oldest in his collection the cover was faded but it still looked beautiful as it was lined with jewels, but what caught my attention was the large, pointed hexagon shaped jewel placed on the middle of the front cover, it looked like the jewel around my neck. The title of the book was the jewel of darkness! Everyone knew about that jewel even non magic users, it was told that it caused darkness to plague the land a long time ago and it brought nothing but pain and death to everyone that carried it. Though it could not be the jewel I had right, I'm sure the magic users would have told me if I had that.

I quickly flicked through the book, it looked like it had all the history and stories on the jewel of darkness with drawings and photos of the different people who carried it throughout the years but what caught my attention was one of the last few pages, it held a photo of the jewel, and it looked exactly like mine and next to that was another two photos, one of a black panther and one of a boy with bright green eyes. I have seen this boy before in another photo and in my dreams, it was Lucas, Tristan's older brother and he was the last person to carry the jewel of darkness before he lost control of the magic stored inside and died.

I sat down on Odin's chair as the news sank in, I was in shock I had the jewel of darkness around my neck, the magical item everyone feared, and it brings death to all who carry it.

I took a deep breath and turned to the next page in the book, my name was there and space to put more details about me and I was numbered, I was the fiftieth person to carry the jewel of darkness and there was clearly a gap on the other pages for the next poor soul to wear the jewel. I remembered seeing Odin going back into the house while I was training, he must have got the book out of one of his boxes as he had wrote down about my eyes zooming in and out like a shapeshifter.

I was angry how could the Mystical Knights hide this from me, I had a right to know the jewel of darkness was wrapped around my neck. It is my life that is in danger and the lives of everyone I care for.

I grabbed the book off the table and ran outside to confront the Mystical Knights.

I held the book up in the air so they could see it and yelled,

"Would someone like to explain this to me?"

Odin's face fell as he noticed what book I held in my hand, and I could tell he never wanted me to see it, my anger started to grow inside me and once again the jewel heated up and turned pure black.

"Rose, calm down we can explain." Said Odin.

"Calm down! How can I calm down, you have all been lying to me this whole time, this jewel isn't just a normal magical item it's the jewel of darkness, people have died wearing this, I have a right to know, you should have told me!" I shouted.

"Why were you in Odin's office? Is it because we are magic users, so you don't trust us." Said Edmund grumpily.

"Edmund!" Shouted Odin as he had noticed sparks appearing from the jewel.

"I did trust you but that is a mistake I won't be making again; I was in his office to get another pencil I didn't realize that was a crime. I thought we were friends, but I obviously mean nothing to all of you, I'm just another number." I threw the book down on the ground then yelled, "Well go ahead and find number fifty-one."

I then pulled the jewel from around my neck and dropped it to the floor, the grass burned where it fell. I turned to leave but someone grabbed my hand, it was Tristan.

"Please Rose let us explain." He said.

"Let go of me." I shouted.

Suddenly we were all pushed into the air by a powerful force of magic that had come from the jewel; we all hit the ground hard. I sat up coughing I was winded; it was hard to breathe.

"Ouch, that hurt." Said Edmund.

I looked up at the others they were all pulling themselves up off the floor, they didn't look badly hurt but Clover had a cut on her head. Marigold also noticed the cut and she looked angry. The others looked scared, I stayed on the floor, the jewel of darkness had floated over to my side and was waiting for me to take it, but I didn't I was too scared to, my anger had got out of control, and I had hurt the Mystical Knights and it could have been worse.

Tristan walked over and sat down beside me there was pain in his eyes as he said,

"My older brother Lucas had the jewel of darkness before you; he was stronger and braver than me. One day he decided to go under cover in the Dark Shadow Guild, it was a risk I didn't want him to take but he did it anyway, he was with them for a week before he came back and told us he had met a girl there called Allena, she was a troubled girl who my brother believed could be persuaded to leave the Dark Shadow Guild and join us but before it could happen their leader found out what was going on, they attacked us and Allena was killed. My brother was so angry he lost control of his magic and it killed him; there was nothing left of him, only dust. So now you know why I don't like to talk about it."

I wiped the tears from my eyes and nodded,

"I'm sorry." I said.

"No, don't apologize Rose, we are the ones who are sorry, you are right we should have told you, but we thought if you knew, the magic would become too much for you and the jewel would react badly. Though keeping it from you was a mistake, I see that now." Said Odin, he bent down and picked up the book. Then he knelt down beside me and said,

"Please take this so you can learn all about the jewel and I will give you my word as a Mystical Knight we will teach you all we know and protect you the best we can, we will help you get through this." The Mystical Knights all nodded in agreement and then Clover came over to me and offered me her hand to help me up, "Don't worry Rose." She said.

I smiled and took her hand, I got to my feet but before I let go of her hand I said,

"I'm sorry about your head Clover."

Before she could reply I felt a sudden pain on my head which made me wince, I dropped her hand, touched my head, and felt blood.

"What…. Just happened?" I asked.

"My word, this has never happened before!" Said Odin, he looked shocked and was looking at Clover's head. I looked at her and noticed why the others were staring, the cut that was once on her head was now gone and it was on my head instead.

"It looks like Rose has just healed Clover but the only

way for her to do it was to transfer the damage to herself." Said Isabella.

"I did…? but I did not do anything, I just felt bad for hurting her." I said as I wiped more blood from the cut. Marigold handed me a tissue and I smiled.

"Thanks."

"Rose, I want you to try something. Close your eyes and concentrate on the wound, feel the pain and the blood, and then make it disappear, pretend the wound has healed." Said Odin.

I nodded then closed my eyes and did what he had told me but no matter on how hard I tried it would not work. I opened my eyes and shrugged.

"It looks like she can only heal other people; I have a sore back you could fix for me." Laughed Edmund.

"Shut up Ed." Smiled Tristan. Edmund grinned back. I looked down at the book in my hand, how much more magic was I going to gain from the jewel I wondered.

"Come on Rose, lets go and clean your head." Said Isabella who had noticed the worried look on my face.

"I think you're forgetting something." Said Marigold who pointed behind me.

I turned around and noticed the jewel was still floating in midair, but now it was glowing blue. I looked at it, not sure of what to do, a big part of me wanted to leave it there.

Tristan saw me hesitate he took the jewel in his hand and held it out to me, I smiled took it then placed it back around my neck.

Chapter 10.
Mirror, Mirror on the wall, Hello Lucas.

It is dark, cold and I'm alone, but I can hear a voice in my head.

"You see Rose; you can't trust them they haven't been telling you the truth, how many more lies will they tell you, how many secrets will they keep from you. Come and join us, I will never lie to you."

It was an unknown voice that sounded like the boy from before who had been wrapped in darkness. I looked around for him but only shadows with red eyes appeared.

I woke up from another nightmare out of breath and scared; the jewel of darkness lit up again around my neck and started to heat up. I took some deep breaths to calm down.

It was still dark outside, but I could hear the birds starting their morning song, so dawn must be approaching. I knew I wasn't going to get back to sleep so I threw on some jeans and a tee-shirt, then sat on the end of my bed thinking of what to do, it was too early for breakfast, and I didn't want to wake the others up.

As I was thinking, something caught my eye in the old mirror hanging on the wall, I stood up, blinked, and looked again. I could see my reflection but someone else was stood behind me I quickly turned around but there was no one there, I was the only one in the room. I looked again at the mirror and there was still two reflections, it was a boy who I had seen before, I gently placed my hand on the glass and the boy smiled.

"Hello Rose, so you can see me." His voice was like an echo.

"What.....Wait are you Lucas?" I asked looking puzzled.

"Yes that is my name." He replied.

"I see I must still be dreaming."

"No, you are awake."

"How is this possible?" I asked.

"It is magic." He laughed.

"Am I doing this with the jewel?" I looked down at the jewel around my neck, but it wasn't glowing.

"In a way yes but it's mostly me, you see I carried the jewel before you and when I went boom, I think a part of my soul attached itself to it. As your magic and strength increases I can now communicate with you but only in dreams and in reflections."

I sat back down on my bed wishing I had stayed asleep, "This is crazy, now I'm talking to dead people." I said.

"Hey, less of the dead I'm still here I haven't gone yet."

I looked up at his bright green eyes, "Sorry but this is kind of a shock to me, can anyone else see you?"

"No, I'm afraid it's just you who can see me, I'm just glad I have someone to talk to, I've been getting bored being by myself." Smiled Lucas.

I suddenly felt an overwhelming sadness and despair, "I'm sorry about what happened to you."

"Hey now, it wasn't your fault and please don't feel sorry for me I had a good life, we don't last forever that's why life is precious but don't worry I will help you the best I can, I won't let you go like I did. Whenever you need advice on the jewel just ask me, I am still a Mystical Knight after all." He smiled then disappeared.

"Lucas?"

There was no reply, maybe he has already had

enough for one day, I shrugged and opened my door
to go out but then I heard him again.
**"Oh, and good luck today, not that you will need it
you are a great rider**."
I turned around to reply but he had gone again, I
smiled and said,
"Thanks Lucas."
I left the room still shocked at the fact I can now talk
to someone who is technically dead, I wonder if he is
the only one I can talk to like that, I thought about my
mother but then quickly shook my head, I can't think
about that right now, Lucas is right, life is precious
and anyway my mother never held the jewel of
darkness, so she wasn't connected to it.

I decided to head outside to see Silver so I quietly tip
toed down the stairs but old houses creek so I am
sure someone must have heard me. I closed the front
door behind me and grabbed Silver's grooming kit out
of the shed before heading out to the fields where he
was staying with the other horses. The warm sun
started to rise higher in the sky; it looked like it was
going to be another lovely day which was good for the
festival. I entered the field Silver was in and closed
the gate behind me then I walked to the middle of the
field, all the horses were at the bottom of the fields
enjoying the longer grass. Silver lifted his head up
and when he noticed it was me, he quickly came
trotting over and nudged me with his soft nose, I
laughed.
"Hello boy, how are you today?"
He neighed and nudged me again and I could tell he
wanted a treat.
"Sorry Silver I have no apples or carrots today, but
would you like a brush instead?"
He turned his head away not happy about not getting

any treats but then he turned back and nudged the brush in my hand.

"Alright if you're good at jumping today I will bring you some apples, does that sound fair?" I laughed.

He neighed his approval and stood still while I brushed him. While I stood brushing the mud from his soft mane I thought back to the events of the day before and what I had learnt about the jewel, the past and Lucas. It was still hard to think about it, I have the jewel of darkness and if I do not learn to control the magic inside, I could end up hurt or worse. I also knew now why the Mystical Knights had kept their distance from me as they were hiding the truth; I just hope they are not hiding anything else from me, I thought.

I know soon I will have to learn all I can about the jewel and study magic but right now I will keep my mind on the show jumping festival. I hadn't even read the book Odin had given me, maybe it was because I didn't want to find out what had happened to the others who had the jewel before me, but I think tonight I will have to start reading it, I need to learn how to control this magic and protect the people I care for, I owe it to myself and Lucas to at least give it a try.

I heard another horse approaching from behind Silver I looked and saw Patrick was making his way over to us.

"Hello Patrick."

He blinked his big brown eyes, opened his mouth then grabbed hold of the brush in my hand. I laughed, I knew he wanted a brush too and was annoyed I was giving Silver all the attention. It's weird but I have always been able to understand what the horses wanted, it is like I can sense it somehow but it's not just with horses I seem to know what all animals need and what they are feeling, and I think that feeling has gotten stronger since I got the jewel, I will have to ask Odin about it later.

I started to brush Patrick which annoyed Silver, "Don't worry Silver; you will be getting my full attention later, you need to look good before we start jumping."

He calmed down and decided to let me groom Patrick while he ate some more grass. I heard the gate open behind me I turned around and saw Tristan was walking towards us.

"Morning." He said.

"Morning, don't tell me you want a brush too." I replied.

He laughed and his face lit up as he stroked Patrick.

"No thanks. He doesn't normally stand still for me you must have the magic touch." He smiled at me.

"Um yeah I guess I do." I said and looked down at the jewel of darkness.

"Are you feeling alright?" He asked as he realized what I was looking at.

"Yeah I'm ok, just tired I didn't sleep well." I replied and stroked Silver on the neck as he ate the grass.

"Are you sure you are alright to ride today?" He asked concerned.

"Yes, don't worry it will help me, anyway I've already told Silver he's jumping today and he's excited, aren't you boy." I smiled.

Silver lifted his head and neighed at Tristan; Tristan smiled.

"Alright if you're sure you are ok then I won't stop you, all of us will be riding to the village together but first we need to go get some breakfast I think Isabella said she was making porridge for us."

Tristan patted Patrick on the neck then started to walk off he then stopped and turned around to make sure I was following him. I patted Silver and Patrick on their

necks then followed Tristan out the field.
As we got closer to the house I asked Tristan a question,
"So, after the jumping festival today do you think it would be alright if I learnt some more magic?"
He looked at me surprised then smiled, "If that's what you want, I'm sure Odin will help you."
I nodded and we entered the small garden. Just before the front door of the house, I spotted something in the small fountain. I stopped and looked closer, it was Lucas's reflection in the water, he smiled and waved at me. I smiled back but didn't wave as Tristan came beside me and asked, "Is something wrong?"
"No, nothing let's go and get some food." I said quickly then opened the front door.

We entered the kitchen and noticed the other Mystical Knights were already sat around the large dining table eating their breakfast. They were all chatting to one another but when they noticed us the room fell silent, great now I feel awkward, I thought.
"Morning." I said then walked over to the sink to wash my hands.
Isabella came over to me and handed me a cup of tea, "Morning Rose, did you sleep well?"
"Thank you." I said and nodded; I knew she could tell by my face that I hadn't slept much.
Odin also walked over to us, "Good morning Rose, are you sure you are well enough to ride today?" He said.
"Yes, I don't want things to change because I have the necklace of death around my neck." I replied grumpily.
Odin flinched and I saw the others stop eating their breakfast to look up at me.

"Sorry, I will be fine." I said then walked over to the table and sat down on one of the empty chairs.
Marigold placed a bowl of porridge in front of me and smiled.
"Thanks." I said and started to eat; the porridge was warm and had a hint of honey on top, it made me feel a little better. I noticed the room was quiet, so I looked up and noticed the others staring at me, but they soon stopped once they saw the annoyed look on my face.
After a while Odin spoke, "Now, today we will all be going to the village together to cheer Rose on and have some fun, we all deserve a break but remember to keep your guard up and bring your weapons as the Dark Shadow Guild could still be lurking about."
Great, now I feel even more nervous, I had not eaten much but I didn't want any more porridge, so I stood up and left the table.
"I'm going to go and get Silver ready." I said then quickly left the room before anyone could say anything.
As the door shut behind me I heard Edmund say, "Great speech old man."
I smiled it sounded like the others knew talking about weapons was a bad idea.
I grabbed a bucket of warm water and Silver's grooming kit that I had left near the door and headed back outside, I put them beside the fence posts then went to fetch Silver from the field. He saw me coming and trotted over to the gate, I smiled and opened the gate to let him out then shut the gate behind him, the other horses looked up but then decided to continue eating the grass.
Silver followed me to the small yard behind the house where I had left the bucket and grooming kit, I grabbed some hay on the way and put it down in a pile for him.

"Here boy, you can have some of this while I get you cleaned up."
Silver huffed happily and got started on eating the hay, as he ate I groomed him the best I could, luckily it wasn't too muddy in the fields, so he wasn't that dirty, so it was easy to get him looking his best for the show.

Once I had finished grooming him I started to plait his mane, while I did, I noticed the Mystical Knights had got their horses from the field and were coming over to groom and tack them up, the other horses were wearing their head collars so they could be tied up to the fence posts to make it easier for the Mystical Knights to get them ready.
After she had finished getting her pony ready, Clover came up to me and said,
"Wow your horse looks pretty in plaits; do you think you can teach me how to plait my horse's mane one day?"
"Yeah of course I can, what's your pony called?" I said as I finished off plaiting Silver's mane.
"She's called Betty." She smiled and gave Silver a pat on the neck. I looked over to where her pony was stood, she was a pretty black mare with a short mane, and she would look stunning in plaits.
"Silver, say hello to Clover." I said.
Silver looked up and started nuzzling Clover's face in greeting, Clover laughed in delight. The other Mystical Knights looked over at us and smiled.
I started to plait Silver's tail while Clover stood and watched with her big gold eyes gleaming.
Odin came over to us and said, "You do have a strong bond with Silver for him to let you do that without having to tie him up."
"Yeah but bribing him with food also helps." I smiled.

Silver turned his head around to look at me; he didn't like what I had said, "Only joking Silver." I laughed. He neighed and turned back around to eat more hay.

"Remarkable, it's like you can both understand each other." Odin said looking puzzled.

"Actually, I was going to ask you about that, I've always been able to understand him, somehow I can sense what he's feeling and what he wants but it's not just with Silver it is like that with all animals, it started when I was little, but I think it has gotten stronger since I got the jewel. So, I was wondering is that a form of magic and is it connected to the jewel of darkness?"

He looked at me confused then replied, "Well I know shapeshifters can communicate with the same animal species that they can turn into. The only other ones who can understand all animals like that is the shapeshifter king and fairy queen, isn't that right Marigold?"

I turned around and noticed Marigold had joined us, "Yes the fairy queen does have a special bond with the animals, no one else can understand them the way she does." She said.

"I think I will have to do some more research on the matter, normally I would have said it was the jewel giving you this power, but you said you've had it before you picked that up, so now I'm not certain, I'm sure it's nothing to worry about though." Explained Odin.

"It's alright, that's one magic power I'm happy to have." I said and smiled at Silver while I put his saddle on.

Odin smiled too, "Yes it is handy, now I think it's time for us to go to the village, why don't you go and get changed we can put Silver's bridle on for you."

"Ok, thanks." I said and went off to change into my

jumping gear.
Once I was ready I quickly made sure I put my dagger into my bag then went back outside to join the others. Odin smiled at me then said, "Right everyone, lets go." We all jumped onto our horses and headed off into the forest.

Chapter 11.
Magic Shield.

Riding through the forest I could tell the Mystical Knights were on high alert for any signs of trouble. They had made sure I was in the middle of the group with Clover so they could keep us safe.

I took a deep breath to try and relax and enjoy the ride, the sun was shining through the tree leaves making the forest sparkle and the flowers smelt fresh. I could hear the birds singing and other creatures in the forest moving about too, at every rustle in the trees I saw Tristan tense up but then calm down when he knew it was not a threat.

As we got closer to the village we started to hear the sounds of the festival, music was playing, children were laughing, men and women were talking, and other horses were neighing in excitement. We could also smell the wonderful food being served. My stomach growled; I knew I should have eaten more porridge for breakfast.

We finally left the forest and entered the village; there were people and horses everywhere having fun. The village looked beautiful with many flowers and flags hanging up around the buildings and stalls that was set up. I was glad we made it without trouble and by the looks on the Knights faces they were too. Tristan though kept glancing at the trees behind us, he saw me looking at him, and he smiled and shrugged his shoulders. Before I could ask him what was wrong I heard someone shout my name.

"Hey, Rose." It was Nick, I jumped off Silver.

"Hello Nick, is everything ready for today?" I asked.

"Yes, everything seems in order, you know how

Anthony gets at events, and my parents are doing fine at the bakery, is everyone else alright?" He asked and looked towards the Mystical Knights.

"Hello Nick, we are all fine thank you." Said Odin as he dismounted his horse.

"Rose, you're here." Shouted Helen who came from behind Nick and gave me a hug.

"Come on, you need to go to the Horse house to get signed in so you can jump, I will take Silver to the waiting area for you." She said and took Silver's reins and walked off.

"There are some stables for the guest's horses to stay, while you enjoy the festival, there are near the farm I will show you; Anthony should still be there helping some others with their horses so he will show you where to put yours. Rose you should go and sign in, Agatha is waiting for you." Said Nick and rolled his eyes.

I smiled we all knew Agatha always took the festival too seriously while trying to impress the minister.

Before the Mystical Knights left to follow Nick they all wished me good luck and Odin said, "We will see you later." I could tell he was annoyed he wasn't coming with me to make sure I stayed safe.

"Don't worry about me I will be fine, go and enjoy yourself you said you needed a break remember." I smiled, waved goodbye and headed off towards the Horse house.

I walked through the door and spotted Agatha sitting behind a small table she had piles of forms in front of her; she looked up and saw me.

"So, you are finally here, I hope you are ready for today, here sign this." She said with a frown and handed me a form.

I took it and signed my name on the line; all the riders

had to do this before they ride to enter the show. I gave the form back to her then walked past the table to enter the second door where the other riders were waiting but before I could go inside the minister walked out.

"Ah, Rose good you are here, I hope being around those nasty magic users haven't ruined how you ride." Said Claudia with a grin.

"If you really believe that then maybe I shouldn't ride and let someone from another village win the trophy this time. And the only one nasty around here is you." I said with anger, I felt the jewel heat up around my neck.

Claudia gasped and I heard Agatha get up from her chair, I quickly pushed passed Claudia and entered the waiting room before I did something I would regret, I was not riding for her or the village anyway, I was doing this for my family at Unicorn Stables and myself. I love to jump with Silver and my mother always loved to watch me, she always said it made her proud and happy, I have won four years in a row, and it always makes more people want to learn to ride at Unicorn Stables, so it makes us more money to look after all the horses we help.

I was not going to let anyone ruin my day.

The Horse house was one room filled with benches in the middle and along one wall, and on the other wall was a row of lockers some riders could use to store their equipment inside, there was also two bathrooms one for women and one for men so the riders could get ready in private. As I was already ready to ride I quickly sat down on one of the benches in the room and took some deep breaths to calm down. I looked down at the jewel, luckily it had stopped glowing, the other riders were on the other side of the room peeping out one of the windows to try and see their friends who were waving at them from outside, they were laughing and talking to each other and looked excited and ready to ride.

I didn't go over and talk with them like I normally would, I was afraid the jewel would react again so I stayed on the bench and pretended I was studying the map of the course we would be jumping when really I was thinking about the jewel and wondering what other magic was stored within it.

As I was thinking I felt someone sit on the bench beside me, I looked up and saw a tall boy about Nick's age or maybe older, he must be a new rider as I did not recognize him from previous festivals. He had black hair and dark blue eyes; he looked at me and smiled.

"Hi, my name is Caleb, this is my first time jumping here I'm a little nervous." He said.

"Hello, I'm Rose, don't worry you will be fine just remember everything you practiced and have fun."

"Wow I'm glad I sat near you; you've helped me already." He smiled again.

I smiled back but before I could say anything else Agatha walked in and shouted out the name of the first rider who would jump, a young girl got up and followed Agatha out the door.

Caleb got up and walked over to another window to look out; one by one the riders were called to jump. We could hear the crowd outside clapping and cheering as the riders finished the course, as they returned to the room some looked happy, but others looked annoyed so maybe they didn't do too well.

Me and Caleb was last to jump, they called my name first which was weird because they normally left me till last as I was the jumper for this village, but they must have changed it, I got up and walked out the door.

Caleb shouted behind me, "Good luck Rose."
"Thanks, you too." I replied.

Silver was waiting for me outside the arena with
Helen.
"Are you sure you're ok to ride, you look tired." She
asked.
I took Silver's reins and gave him a pat on the neck,
"Yes I'm fine don't worry."
"Alright, well good luck not that you will need it I'm
sure you will do great like always." She smiled as I
climbed onto Silver's back; I nodded and rode into the
arena.
We walked around the jumps, and I spotted the
Mystical Knights in the crowd waving at me, I smiled
at them then walked Silver over to the judges and
bowed, Silver bowed too he is a smart horse, and he
knew what he was doing, the judges smiled, and the
crowd cheered. One of the judges ran a bell to tell me
it was time to start; we set off trotting then cantered
over the first jump. As we needed to do it in a good
time we quickened our pace over the second jump,
there were eight jumps in total and Silver jumped over
them all perfectly, we didn't knock any poles down
and we were fast. After the last jump the crowd
cheered again, I laughed and gave Silver another pat.
"You were great boy." I said.
He neighed to tell me he knew he was, we both love
jumping together.
After bowing again at the judges, we left the arena, I
jumped off Silver and Helen came over to take his
reins again as she had to take him back to his stable.
"That was great; I think you might be in the lead
again." She smiled.
"Thank you Helen." I said, and she walked off with
Silver.

I had to go back to the Horse house and wait for the judges to decide who had won but when I got back only Caleb was waiting.

"So, your back, how did it go?" He asked.

"We did great, where are the other riders I thought we all had to wait here until the judges called us again?" I said and looked back at the door I had entered.

"I don't know, I think they were saying something about going to see the horses, they all just left." Replied Caleb.

"That's weird, they normally can't wait to hear the results, it's strange they would all just leave." I sat down near him.

"Yes it is strange isn't it; while we wait for the others to return, I was wondering who gave you that necklace?" He said and pointed at my neck.

I looked down to make sure it was not glowing, "My mother gave me the chain and I found the jewel, well my dog did, why do you ask?" Something suddenly did not feel right.

"Oh, no reason it just looks special and important to you." He smiled.

"Yeah I guess it is special." I laughed.

"Would it be alright if I had a closer look?" He held out his hand.

My hand touched the jewel, would it be alright to let him hold it, I thought. Before I could take it off my neck I spotted something in the mirror on the wall behind him, I could see Lucas again he was waving his arms about and shaking his head looking worried, I heard his voice in my head.

"Rose Run!"

I quickly stood up, "Sorry I have to go." I turned to leave but before I could go, Caleb grabbed my arm.

"What's wrong Rose don't you trust me? I only wanted

to have a look."

"I….." I wasn't sure how to answer, something was definitely wrong, Lucas wanted me to run and why hadn't Caleb been called out to jump.

"I think my friends are waiting outside." I said and tried to pull my arm away, but he held on tight.

"You're not going anywhere Rose; you're staying here with me, or you can hand over your jewel and leave instead." He smirked.

"Who are you?" I shouted.

"I told you my name, but I didn't tell you I'm the leader of shadows."

I suddenly heard screaming and people shouting outside, then beside me shadow demons appeared. I pulled my arm away from Caleb, but the shadows grabbed hold of me, their hands felt cold, and their red eyes gleamed with anger and hate.

Caleb walked towards me and held his hand out towards the jewel.

"Nooooooo!" I screamed then used my magic and pushed Caleb and the demons away from me, they all slammed against the walls, before I could get my magic back under control, another shadow latched onto my arm with its sharp teeth which caused me to lose control and a large burst of magic power caused one side of the building to collapse and the shadow turned to dust with a howl.

I quickly grabbed my dagger from my bag then ran outside, I felt dizzy, but I had to help everyone.

All around me shadow demons were chasing the villagers and other guests from the festival, they were screaming, and children were crying. I saw Silver leading the other horses to safety, so I tried to make my way to him, as I ran the shadows kept trying to grab me, so I kept using my dagger and powering it with my magic just like Odin had with his sword to make the demons vanish. I spotted the Mystical Knights fighting off demons and trying to help the other people into the village hall to keep them safe, I looked over again at Silver and the horses and realized they were moving into the forest so I stopped to catch my breath, the shadows were not chasing the horses only the humans so it looked like they would be fine.

I decided to turn right and head towards the village hall to help the others, it was difficult as the shadows still kept coming and my energy was low, but I kept going. Tristan was the first one by my side.

"Are you alright Rose?" He said but then noticed the gash on my arm where the shadow had bit me and he looked worried.

"I'm alright, what about you?"

"Don't worry about me I've been in tougher fights." He smiled then used his sword to knock a demon away.

"This is fun, right guys." A blast of fire took out three nearby shadows as Edmund came to stand beside us.

Odin shouted, "Rose get to the village hall we will take care of this."

"No, I have to help you!" I yelled back.

"Don't be stupid, you have to keep the jewel safe." He yelled back as he took out another shadow.

I was about to argue back but I saw James, Jack and Hannah trying to get to the village hall with a demon chasing them, so I ran as fast as I could towards them and blasted out more magic and took out the demon.

"Are you all ok?" I asked them.

"Yeah." Said James but they wouldn't come any closer, they kept glancing at me as we neared the village hall, I could see fear in their eyes, and I wasn't sure if they were more afraid of me or the shadows.

Helen and Anthony ran from behind the hall and met up with us; Hannah ran to Helen and gave her a hug.
"All of you get inside!" Shouted Isabella who was behind us.
We turned and saw a lot more shadows appearing from the forest, the Mystical Knights had also gathered in front of the hall and were getting ready to defend it. Anthony, Helen, Hannah, Jack, and James ran inside but I hesitated,
"You too Rose." Said Odin who had noticed me stop.
Isabella saw me shake my head, so she said, "You need to protect your friends inside right, don't worry about us this is what we train for."
Tears welled up in my eyes as I turned to go inside.
"Don't die." I said before entering the hall.

The hall was full, everyone was packed in looking scared, some children were crying but everyone else was trying to stay quiet so they could hear what was going on outside. A few villagers were trying to look out of the windows when I entered, they turned to face me, and Sheriff Gordon asked.
"Is it safe yet?"
I shook my head.
"Damn this doesn't look good." Said another man who was stood at a window looking out.
"I knew having magic users in the village would bring trouble." Said Claudia.
I saw some of the other villagers nod in agreement, so I stayed quiet; I spotted Nick next to his parents he was hugging his mother looking worried, he saw me and smiled. I then saw Willow looking pale and sitting near the doctor, the other Unicorn members were also stood around her, so I went over to make sure she was alright.
Willow saw me coming, "Oh Rose I'm glad you're

safe." She said then started coughing. The doctor handed her a bottle of water, and she took a sip. "Yeah I'm alright, what about you, are you ok?" I asked.

She smiled and nodded then had another drink; the doctor looked at her worried. I was about to ask him what was wrong when I noticed something in the mirror on the wall, it was Lucas again, so I walked over to it to see what he wanted.

"Rose, more shadows are coming, and it may be too much for the others to handle, there is a way you can help them, but it may be difficult." He said.

"What do I need to do?" I asked him.

Lucas smiled, **"There is a magic shield you can put around everyone but it's tricky, it took me a few months to master the spell."**

"Just show me how to do it and I will try my best." I said.

"Rose, who are you talking to?" Asked Helen who had come beside me looking worried.

I looked around the room and noticed everyone was staring at me, oops, I thought. I blushed and replied, "I will explain later."

I turned back to Lucas and nodded; he grinned and then showed me how to cast the spell of protection. He knelt down and put his hand to the floor then said, **"You need to connect to the earth's magic energy, let it flow through you, then imagine a wall or a glass dome going up around the ones you care for, the harder you concentrate the stronger and bigger the shield will become. The magic will stop the shadow demons and it should stay up a while to protect everyone."**

"Right, that doesn't sound too hard." I nodded and smiled.

"Yeah its a piece of cake, now go and show those

shadows who's in charge." He laughed.

I nodded and turned to leave but before I could, some of the villagers near the windows started to shout.

"Some more are coming." Said Noah who had joined them at the window.

I quickly headed towards the door, but Helen grabbed my arm, luckily the one that wasn't injured and said, "What are you doing? You can't go out there it's too dangerous."

"Helen don't worry I will be alright, I have a way to stop the shadows and keep everyone safe, but I need to go outside." I said and pulled my arm from her grip.

"No, you don't; this isn't your job they're the Mystical Knights not you, I mean you're injured and you're talking to yourself that isn't normal." She said as tears welled up in her eyes as she looked at the blood on my other arm.

I took hold of her hands and said,

"I'm fine, I don't have time to explain please trust me, I promise you I will come back but I need to save everyone first. If you had an idea to help, you would not hesitate you would already be out of the door, so please let me go."

Helen let go of my hands then nodded, "Fine just come back alive."

"Try to keep everyone else inside when I leave." I quickly said then ran out of the door before anyone else could stop me, luckily the others were all trying to watch out of the windows, to even realize I had left which was good because I needed everyone to stay in one place for this plan to work.

The Mystical Knights were still standing after fighting off the first lot of shadows, but they looked tired, and Tristan had changed into his panther form. They all turned around when they heard the door close behind me.

"What are you doing, get back inside." Shouted Odin.

I shook my head, "Sorry I can't do that; besides, I have an idea."

I quickly ran forward to get in front of the Mystical Knights.

"Rose! Come back." Yelled Isabella.

I stopped as Tristan had ran in front of me and he was snarling.

"Don't worry I'm not going any further." I said.

He still wouldn't move, and he kept snarling.

"Damn it Tristan, don't blame me it was your brother's idea." I shouted.

He stopped snarling and looked puzzled, before he could recover and before anyone else could stop me, I quickly ran in front of Tristan, knelt down, and slammed my hand to the ground and did what Lucas had told me.

I felt a strong connection to the earth's magic, it felt warm and alive; I smiled as I imagined the shield in my mind and the jewel lit up a bright green.

"Don't try and stop her Tristan, she could lose control of her magic!" I heard Odin yell, but I didn't stop.

I concentrated hard and my magic became stronger. The shield built up all around the village, it was a glass dome that sparkled a bright green, the shadows that were coming from the forest gave a horrible cry and tried to run faster to get past the shield, but it was too late, the magic barrier was up and no monster could penetrate it, the demons that hit the wall melted away and the ones left behind disappeared into the shadows.

I saw Caleb near the trees; he waved and then disappeared into the forest.

The Mystical Knights looked shocked as they stared at the shield around us.

I smiled and said.
"Piece of cake." Then I closed my eyes and passed out.

Chapter 12.
I hear the voice of my friend.

I woke up in a field full of flowers, there was a large mirror in front of me and Lucas walked out of it. "What happened, did I fall down a rabbit hole?" I smiled.

Lucas laughed, **"You did well Rose everyone is safe now."**

I stood up and there was a throbbing pain in my head, "Ouch, I know this is a dream so why does my head hurt?" I said as I rubbed my forehead.

"Sorry Rose but your head will be sore for a while, that's what happens when you use too much earth magic at once. There is always a price to pay when using strong magic." He said and sat down on a log that was near us.

I sat down beside him, "Well give me a little warning next time."

"You put up a great shield for your first attempt, I knew you could protect the village hall, but you managed to protect the entire village. Even I couldn't shield such a large area, the jewel is responding well to you."

"Well, I had a great teacher, though I might have a problem when I wake up, I told the others it was your idea." I told him.

Lucas nodded, **"I know, I saw the look on my brother's face, it can't be helped, sooner or later you would have had to tell them about me. I think it's time they knew the truth."**

"Alright. If they ask I will explain everything I know, though I still don't really know how it's possible myself."

"Don't worry I'm sure you will manage, your

stronger than me after all." Said Lucas and he stood up and started walking back towards the mirror.
"Lucas thanks for the help, you really are the best Mystical Knight."
Lucas smiled, walked back into the mirror, and vanished.

I opened my eyes, I was in a bed back at Old House with the Mystical Knights sat around me, and they all had worried looks on their faces.
"Don't worry I'm not dead yet." I smiled and sat up, my head felt worse, and the room spun.
"Do you think this is a joke! You could have been killed using a spell that strong, what the hell were you thinking? And how did you know how to do that?" Yelled Odin.
"Ow, please don't shout my head is killing me. I would use that spell again if it meant saving the lives of my family and friends, I thought you would be happy you didn't have to fight anymore." I said as I rubbed my head. My arm was sore too and I noticed it had been bandaged up.
"You think we would be happy if you were to die, we have already lost too many people because of that jewel, now are you going to answer my question, how did you know how to use that spell?" Odin said angrily.
"Um, well it's difficult to explain." I said and glanced at Tristan, should I really tell them the truth? Should I tell them about Lucas? I thought.
"Helen said, 'before you ran out of the village hall you were talking to yourself looking at a mirror,' does that have something to do with it?" Asked Isabella.
"Are Helen and the others ok? What about the horses?" I asked.
"Everyone is fine and so are the horses, they came

back to the village once the trouble stopped, they didn't have any problems walking back through your shield." Explained Isabella.

"You mentioned my brother, you said it was his idea, can you explain that?" Said Tristan who looked annoyed.

Alright. Lucas was right it looks like I can't hide the truth forever and maybe the Mystical Knights deserve to know; Lucas was a part of their family after all, but how do I explain? I can hear your dead brother and see him and will they even believe me. I took a deep breath, well maybe I should start from the beginning. I pointed at the mirror I could see on the wall opposite the bed I was in,

"When everyone looks in a mirror, what do you all see?" I asked.

The Mystical Knights looked at the mirror puzzled; they probably thought something was going to happen.

"We see our reflections." Smiled Clover.

Good someone understood me.

I smiled, "Yes that's right, I see my reflection too but sometimes I can see someone else with me."

"Someone else?" Odin looked at me worried.

I looked at Tristan, "I can see and hear Lucas."

"What! How is this possible?" Said Odin, the Mystical Knights looked shocked.

"Well Lucas believes when he passed away a part of his soul attached itself to the jewel, he doesn't know how it happened or why, but he's been helping me all this time. I guess he still wants to be a Mystical Knight." I smiled at Lucas in the mirror.

"Well, I've never heard of any magic like this, I'm not sure what to make of it." Said Odin.

"Rose can you only see him in mirrors?" Asked Isabella.

"No, anything that reflects images work, but mirrors are clearer. I can also talk to him through my dreams and sometimes when I've been in trouble I've heard his voice in my head." I replied.

"Well, that's weird." Said Edmund who had been unusually quiet.

"I think we need to find out more about this kind of magic I will contact some of our friends to ask for help, Isabella can you check through our books and see if any of them mention this?" Said Odin.

"Of course." She replied.

"There is no need, we all know what's going on but you're just afraid to admit it." Said Tristan angrily.

"What are you talking about?" Asked Odin.

"It's obviously the Dark Shadow Guild using some kind of trick to get Rose to follow them, Lucas is dead, we all saw it there wasn't even a body left for us to bury!" Shouted Tristan.

The other Mystical Knights fell silent, I looked towards the mirror not sure of what to say.

Lucas said, "**You have to make them believe it's really me.**"

I shrugged how was I supposed to do that, I could tell they were all upset.

"**Tell Tristan when we were younger we went exploring around the palace grounds, we were both hiding from our teacher as we didn't want to be stuck inside studying when it was such a nice day and as we hid we both discovered a secret space only us two know about, we decided it would become our hideout when we needed our space from others we would go there and relax. We never told anyone else about it.**" He said.

Tears welled up in Lucas's eyes as he remembered and in my eyes as I felt his sadness.

"It is Lucas, I never got to meet him when he was

alive, but I know it's definitely him, he's been helping
me, he showed me how to use the spell of protection,
it took him three months to learn it." I said and before
Tristan could interrupt me I told him the story Lucas
had told me.

The other Mystical Knights looked at Tristan; there
was a long pause as the news sunk in. Tristan stood
up and said,

"It is Lucas." Then he quickly left the room, Edmund
got up to follow him, but Odin stopped him. "Leave
him be for a bit he's had a shock, we all have. Rose
why didn't you tell us sooner?"

"I'm sorry, I wasn't sure myself at first if it was real or
just something I had made up in my head and then
Lucas told me it would be best not to tell you because
he knew it would upset you. And I was also worried
you would think I've gone crazy and take me away
somewhere, I was scared, sorry." The tears fell from
my eyes.

Odin smiled at me, then held my hand, "My dear, we
are here to help you no matter what, that's our job as
Mystical Knights but also your friends and in time we
may even become a family. So, for us to help you
please don't hide things from us or not tell us what
effects the jewel is having on you because it will
become harder for us to do our jobs and learn all we
can about the jewel and its magic. Tell Lucas if he still
wants to be a Mystical Knight he needs to remember
that."

I wiped away my tears and nodded then looked at
Lucas, he had the biggest grin on his face.

"Don't worry he heard you, he said yes sir and
saluted." I told them and smiled.

Odin suddenly looked upset, "Are you alright?" I
asked.

"I'm sorry I didn't realize he could hear us, I assumed

only you could talk to him." Odin looked at the mirror and said, "We have missed you Lucas."

Again tears welled up in my eyes just like Lucas as the other Mystical Knights gathered around the mirror and told him how much they miss him and apologized for not saving him.

"He doesn't blame anyone for what happened to him, and he doesn't want anyone blaming themselves either, sometimes bad things happen and there is nothing you can do about it, but he's going to try his best to make sure it doesn't happen again." I said as I repeated what Lucas told me.

The others nodded and Odin stood up and looked at me.

"Right, we better leave and let Rose get some rest, using earth magic isn't easy and even though she won't admit it I can tell she's tired. She's stubborn just like Lucas." He smiled.

I smiled back and laid my head back down on the pillow, he was right I was exhausted, my eyes started to close as I watched the Mystical Knights leave the room.

When I woke up again the sun was rising and I was alone in the room, I must have slept through the whole night. I sat up, my head felt better but I still felt weak, and my arm was still sore, I was also hungry, so I climbed out of bed, had a wash, and changed into some clean clothes before I headed downstairs to find food.

I entered the kitchen and noticed I was the first one up; the rest of the house was quiet, so I made some toast and a cup of coffee and sat down at the kitchen table. I placed the small handheld mirror I had brought with me from Unicorn Stables on the table beside me then started to eat.

"Take it easy Rose, you will make yourself ill eating that fast." Said Lucas who had appeared in the mirror.

I looked down at him and swallowed a mouth full of toast.

"I can't help it I'm hungry, is it because I used too much magic?" I asked him.

"Yes, it used to happen to me all the time, you will get used to it, just take your time eating and save some for the others." He laughed.

"Alright I will try." I laughed and took another bite.

The kitchen door opened, and Tristan walked in, he stopped when he noticed me, and he looked like he was about to turn around, but Edmund pushed him in.

"You need to eat, morning Rose I hope you have saved some food for us, using magic is hard work, I'm starving." Said Edmund.

"Morning, don't worry I saved you some. So, using magic makes you hungry too?" I asked.

"Yeah it's like that with everyone, if you want to know who works the hardest at H.Q. it's the cooks, they are always making food for someone." Replied Edmund as he started cooking some eggs and bacon. I looked at Tristan who had sat down with a glass of milk.

"H.Q.?" I asked.

"Oh, it's what we call our home sometimes." Edmund smiled.

"Oh right, I remember my mother telling me the Mystical Knights live in a large house near the kings castle, is that true?"

"Yep it's true, the Mystical Knights live together with the magic item users, keeping them under one roof helps to keep them safe and it's easier for us." Said Edmund.

The room fell silent as I realized what he had just said, does that mean I would have to leave my home and go live with them.

"Oh, don't worry not everyone has to live there with us, could you help me make the toast?" Said Edmund, I could tell he was trying to change the subject.

"Um right." I said and started putting some slices of bread in the oven, I glanced at Tristan, he looked annoyed, and he hadn't said one word to me, he would barely even look at me.

"Would you like some toast too Tristan?" I asked him.

"Um, yeah thanks." He said, glanced at me then drank some more milk.

As the toast cooked I helped Edmund put some of the pots away in the cupboard.

"Thank you Rose, you've been a big help." He said.

"I haven't done that much." I smiled.

"Well, you've done more than him." Said Edmund pointing a finger at Tristan who growled in reply.

I smiled and took the toast out of the oven; I put two slices on a plate for Edmund then put a lot of butter and bacon on two more slices for Tristan, as I had heard Lucas's voice in my head telling me how he likes his toast.

I put the plate in front of Tristan then sat down opposite him to finish off my cup of coffee. Tristan stared at the plate in front of him.

"Don't just stare; eat it up before it gets cold." Said Edmund who sat next to him with his plate of toast, eggs, and bacon. He smiled as he noticed the way I had made Tristan's toast.

I could tell me being there was making Tristan feel uncomfortable, so I stood up and said. "I'm going out for a walk."

"Alright but don't go too far." Said Edmund as I walked out the door.

I got outside and took a deep breath of fresh air; the bright warm sun was high in the sky again and the birds were singing happily.
I looked down at the mirror in my hand that I had brought with me, while I walked and said,
"I don't think your brother likes me."
"Of course he does, who wouldn't like someone like you. He's just annoyed he can't see or hear me too; he probably wants to get angry at me for leaving him. And I think he just needs time to figure out what to say to you, he's always been like that, I'm sure he will talk to you soon maybe after he's finished eating his toast." Said Lucas who smiled in the mirror.
"Alright, well I will give him some space." I smiled.
I understood what Lucas was saying I would find it difficult too, if my mother had suddenly appeared in a mirror but I couldn't talk to her and only Tristan could, I wouldn't know how to react either.
I got to the area where the new stables would be built, the Mystical Knights had done a good job of clearing the area, so it was all ready for Noah to bring the supplies and start building them. I knew Helen and the others were alright, but something was bothering me about the way they looked at me yesterday, they had fear in their eyes but it wasn't the shadows they were looking at, it was me.
Maybe they blamed me for the shadows attacking everyone too and maybe they are right to blame me, the jewel was around my neck after all.
I sat down on the grass but this time I kept my distance from the forest, my arm ached as I remembered the shadow biting me.
After a while I saw Odin and Tristan coming towards me, they were both carrying swords and Tristan held a large bag.

"Ah there you are Rose; Good Morning are you feeling any better?" Said Odin.

"Morning, yes I'm alright." I replied.

"Good, if you're up for it we would like you to learn how to use a sword; we think it would be a good idea, as you can't always use your magic because your energy will become dangerously low. It's your decision though; we wouldn't force you to do something you don't want to do." Odin said with a smile.

I looked at Tristan and he also smiled at me, so I stood up.

"Ok, if you think it's a good idea I will try but I'm warning you I can be clumsy sometimes." I said.

Odin laughed, "That's why you won't be using the real swords to practice." He held out his hand and Tristan handed him a wooden sword from the bag he was carrying. Odin looked at it then handed it to me.

"Right, I will leave this to you Tristan; I have other jobs to do." He said, then started walking away back towards the house.

Before he got too far he turned around and shouted, "Don't hurt Tristan too badly."

"I will try my best." I smiled.

Odin continued to walk towards the house, but I could hear him laughing. I glanced at Tristan beside me; he put the bag and his real sword down on the ground then took another wooden sword from the bag. Then he stood in front of me and said,

"Thanks for the toast."

"You're welcome. So now what, do I have to try and hit you?" I smiled.

"First I need to show you how to stand, which hand do you use?" He asked.

"My right." I replied and held out the sword.

"Ok me too. So, before you learn how to fight you

127

need to know how to stand correctly so you don't lose your balance, like this." He said and got into a stance. He had his right foot forward with his hand holding the sword, and his left foot was further behind.
"I've learnt to use one hand holding my sword but it's best to hold your sword with two hands to begin with." He put the sword in both hands and showed me how to stand, I did what he did.
"Right, that's it, now I want you to swing the sword like this."
He stepped forward and his wooden blade cut through the air from left to right, then he stepped again, and it cut from right to left. He did this twice then nodded at me.
I copied his movements, everyone in the village gets taught how to use a dagger because of the dangerous creatures that lurk in the forest, you must know how to defend yourself in case you run into one. Not everyone is good at it though and some of the villagers have even decided to stop learning how to use one and just make sure they have someone with them who knows how to use one instead, but my mother made sure I knew how to defend myself she always said it was important, so I was alright at using one if I needed to, but I never did, and Silver normally scared anything away that was a threat.
Using the wooden sword felt different it was heavier and longer and you had to balance it just right in your hand so you wouldn't drop it, but the more I practiced the easier it became, and I started to get used to it.
We continued to practice for a while and Tristan showed me different sword techniques, how to defend and attack.
"Good, that will do for today you can keep the wooden sword, keep practicing the moves I've shown you and you should get good in no time, lets go back to the

house and get something to drink." Said Tristan and he started to walk off.

"Wait…Um Lucas wants to tell you something." I said as he stopped.

He didn't turn around, but he said, "**I knew this was a bad idea.**"

"If you thought it was a bad idea then don't do it, I'm not forcing anyone to teach me or protect me. Just go home I can take care of myself; I don't need any knights in shining armor to help me." I said angrily and pushed passed him to walk off on my own.

Tristan grabbed my hand, "Wait, how did you know I was thinking that?"

"What are you talking about?" I said and pulled my hand away.

"I…. Just now I thought this was a bad idea, in my head." He said looking confused.

"Yes I know I heard you; did I whack you on your head with my sword or something." I looked at him puzzled.

"That's my point Rose, I didn't say anything."

"What? I don't understand."

"Wait, I'm going to think of something, and I want you to see if you can hear me."

"Alright now you're freaking me out." I said and backed away.

"Just do it." Tristan stared at me with intense green eyes, and then said.

"**Rose.**"

I blinked somehow he had said that without moving his lips, I heard his voice again. "**So did you hear me?**"

"**Wait, What, how?**" I thought.

He smiled, "**So we can both communicate with each other through our minds.** He thought.

I looked down at the jewel around my neck, it did not look any different.

"It's called the mental link, it's a magic that can let people communicate with each other through their minds by thinking to each other, it is strange how we can do it though, it's a rare gift normally only really close friends or family members can do it." Tristan said aloud and sat down on the grass.

He looked more shocked than I was, I sat down near him and put my head in my hands I wasn't sure how much more magic I could deal with.

"Are you alright?" He asked.

"Yeah, I guess I have to be more careful about what I think from now on." I laughed.

"No, it doesn't work like that, I can't read your mind and you can't read mine; it only works if you want me to hear you then I will. It's an old magic and rare no one knows for sure how it works, I could do it with Lucas…." Tristan paused and looked at the mirror I had put on the floor between us with my wooden sword.

I also looked down and I could see Lucas laughing.

"Wait is this because of you?" I asked him.

He shrugged his shoulders and continued to laugh,

"He's laughing at us." I told Tristan.

He blushed and stood up, "Come on let's go." He said then walked off quickly towards the house. I stood up and ran to catch up to him.

As we got closer to the house I heard a familiar sound of horse hooves running towards me, I stopped and turned around and saw Silver. He stopped in front of me and started to rub his head against my arm though I had to move it out the way as it had become sore again, training with Tristan probably had not helped my wound.

"Hello boy, I've missed you too." I laughed and patted him on the neck. I noticed he had a ribbon with a pouch attached to his neck, I knew it held a note inside. Tristan looked confused so I explained to him, "Silver somehow manages to find me wherever I am when no one else can find me or are too busy to come themselves, so when anyone needs me they attach notes to him, and he delivers them." I pulled the note from the pouch and read it; my heart skipped a beat it was not good news.

Chapter 13.
Bad News.

Silver knew what I wanted he bent his head down so I could grab his mane and jump up onto his back, but before I could go Tristan stepped in front of us.

"Wait, what's wrong where are you going?" He asked.

"I have to go back to Unicorn Stables, Willow is not well, and it must be serious for them to tell me like this, they need me."

"Alright, but I'm coming with you let me go and get Patrick. Wait there." He said then ran off to get his horse ready.

Once Tristan was ready we took off, we got through the forest without trouble. Silver and Patrick ran fast and without a saddle or bridle I had to hold onto Silver's mane and keep my balance, he could tell I was worried and needed to get home.

The note I had received sounded bad; it had read.

'Come Home Now! Willow not well, we need you. From Hannah.'

The fact that Hannah had to write the note and attach it to Silver must have meant the others were too busy looking after Willow.

We arrived at Unicorn Stables and jumped off our horses, we were greeted by Abbey the Doctors assistant. She was dressed smartly like always and her long brown hair was plaited and tied up in a bun, she had a sad expression on her face when she came to see us.

"Ah hello Rose, I will take care of your horses, the doctor is with Willow, you should go and see her now." She said and the look in her eyes made me feel nervous.

I nodded and said, "Thank you."

We left Silver and Patrick with Abbey then ran into the house, we could hear voices coming from upstairs, so we headed up. There was a crowd of people outside Willow's room, a few from the village and the Unicorn members. Hannah spotted me first and ran over to give me a hug; I could tell she had been crying.
"I didn't think you would come." She said.
"Have I not told you before, if you need me, no matter where I am, I will come. Now what's wrong, is Willow alright?" I asked.
Hannah shook her head and looked like she was going to cry again. I glanced at Tristan who was still beside me; he shrugged his shoulders not knowing what to say. Another voice came from the crowd,
"Ah Rose you are here, could you come with me please, your friend can come too." Said Doctor Thomas.
Before I followed him back down the stairs I looked back down at Hannah, she nodded then ran back to Nick's parents who I spotted talking to Noah, I couldn't see Nick though.
I followed the doctor with Tristan close behind me and we entered the office. Nick was sat waiting for us he smiled and waved but he didn't speak, and he looked sad. Doctor Thomas closed the door behind us then turned around to talk, "Now, I've called you both in here to explain to you what's wrong with Willow, Nick already knows the details." He turned to Nick who nodded at him then he took a deep breath and continued.
"Rose I know you don't know about this, but Willow has been unwell for a while now, she has a bad heart which causes her to feel weak and tired."
"What! Why wouldn't she say anything about this?" I asked but I already knew the answer.
"She didn't want anyone to worry, though I think

Helen knew something was wrong, as she has been telling her to rest more which was the right thing to do. And that was helping along with the medication she was taking, however due to the events that took place at the festival it has become a lot worse, the stress of that day put too much pressure on her heart and now the medication is no longer working." He stopped to let the news sink in, I looked towards Nick he had his head in his hands and he would not look at me.

I looked back at the doctor and asked, "Well you can find her some more medication right, something else that might work."

"No Rose, I'm sorry it is too late for that; she has become too weak and I'm afraid she hasn't got much time left."

Tears welled up in my eyes as I remembered the last time the doctor had told me that. "No, it can't be right; they must be something else we can do."

"The only thing we can do is make her last moments as comfortable as we can." Said the doctor.

"But….."

Nick got to his feet, walked towards me, and gave me a hug, he said.

"There is nothing else we can do Rose but see her off with a smile on our faces." I buried my head in his arm not believing what I was hearing, Willow cannot leave us. I heard a voice in my head, but it was not Lucas it was Tristan.

"I'm sorry Rose."

Then an idea came to me, and I shouted, "Magic, that's it!" And I ran out of the room before the others could stop me, but Tristan knew what I was thinking even without me telling him through our mind link. He was faster than the doctor and Nick; he grabbed hold of my hand and shouted.

"Don't you dare that is never going to work!"

"It will, don't you remember what happened with Clover?" I pulled away from his grasp.

"That was different that was a scratch not a bad heart or old age." He said.

"So what, it still might work." I told him as we walked up the stairs.

"Are you crazy even if it did work the only way you can heal someone is by taking the damage yourself, you can't go around with a bad heart when the Dark Shadow Guild is after you, it will only make you an easier target."

"That is why you are here, to protect me. That's what the Mystical Knights are for."

"Even we can't be with you every second of every day."

I turned around to face him, "Please Tristan I have to try something, wouldn't you if it was for someone you cared for?" More tears welled up in my eyes and I quickly wiped them away and started to walk towards Willow's room.

"I'm sorry Rose but I still can't let you take that risk." He said as he followed me.

I spun around with anger, "And how are you going to stop me?" I shouted and I felt the jewel heat up.

"Rose!" Tristan growled angrily and his eyes lit up a darker shade of green.

Nick put a hand on his shoulder and said, "It's alright Tristan let her go, she needs to go and see Willow, she will make her understand."

Tristan heaved a sigh and nodded, "Fine." He said.

Nick and the doctor had been following us this whole time and when I turned around I noticed the others outside Willow's room had also been listening to us.

I took a deep breath to calm down, then headed towards Willow's room, Helen held the door open for me and said,

"She has been waiting for you Rose, she would like to see you too Tristan."

Tristan looked puzzled but nodded and followed me into the room, the doctor also followed us in; Helen stayed outside the room with the others and shut the door behind us.

Willow was lying down in her bed that was next to the window, the window was open wide to let some fresh air in. The doctor stayed near the door and nodded towards Willow, the room wasn't large so not many people could fit in all at once, that's why the others decided it would be best to visit her in small groups, we had done it once before when she had caught a cold, we would take turns and look after her, but this was definitely worse.

As Tristan and I got closer to her bed I realized how pale and unwell she was and she somehow looked smaller, her breathing was shallow and slow. I glanced at Tristan beside me he was looking at Willow with sad eyes; we both knew it was not good news.

"Well don't just stand there children, come closer I don't bite." She said as her eyes flickered open. She moved a bit to try and sit up, but she started coughing, I quickly got her the glass of water from the small table beside her bed and helped her drink, she took a sip then laid her head back down on the pillow. She was tired and it was the weakest she had ever looked, why had I not noticed sooner she must have been hiding it for a long time. Tears welled up in my eyes as I held her hand, I could feel the jewel around my neck heating up. Tristan put his hand on my shoulder and said,

"Magic won't work here Rose, so please don't try, it's too dangerous."

"I have to.....I."

"Now that's enough Rose." Willow said angrily.
Then with a gentler voice she continued, "Your
mother and I taught you better than that, do you not
remember what she told you the day she died."
I nodded.
"Then tell me, what did she say?" Willow asked.
"She said when someone's time is up in this world no
amount of magic can heal nor bring them back from
death and that is why life is precious, that is why we
need to live the best we can, while we can, so when
the time has come we can smile and laugh onto the
other side and keep watch over the ones we love
without regrets and see the world from a different
view point." I smiled at Willow as the tears fell from
my eyes. Willow squeezed my hand tighter and said,
"You have had a difficult life Rose and it's probably
going to get a lot harder, I'm sorry I won't be with you
to help but I have taught you everything I know, and
you have new friends now to guide you on your new
path." She looked towards Tristan then back at me
and continued,
"Now remember to keep that beautiful smile on your
face and stay strong, let your heart guide you and
trust your instincts. I know you won't let darkness
win." She lifted her hand and touched the jewel
around my neck,
"Do not let your precious light fade." She smiled.
I nodded and wiped away my tears then I gave Willow
a hug, I did not know what to say so I just held her in
my arms.
After a while Willow let go of me and said, "Right, off
you go you two, I'm sure you have a lot of work to do,
ah Tristan before you go can you give something to
Robert for me?" She nodded at Doctor Thomas, he
walked over to Tristan and handed him a letter.
"Of course." Said Tristan and he placed the letter in

his pocket.

"Tristan thank you for taking such good care of Rose, I'm glad you have become such good friends, I hope she can count on you in the future." Said Willow.

Tristan blushed, "Um sure…. You have my word I will keep her safe."

Willow smiled at us both then closed her eyes, "Could you send Anthony and Helen in to see me." She said quietly.

I looked at the doctor, he nodded and opened the door for us to leave but before I left the room I turned around and said,

"Thank you for everything Willow, goodbye."

"Not goodbye Rose, see you later." She said.

I smiled, "Yeah see you soon." Then the door closed behind me.

Chapter 14.
Goodbye.

"She's gone."

Those were the words Anthony spoke when he came back out of Willow's room just a few minutes after he had entered with Helen. We had all been sat in silence outside her door waiting, but once those words were spoken the Unicorn members grieved for their loss. The others had stayed together to comfort each other but I walked outside alone, the jewel around my neck felt heavy and my heart was in pain, the tears fell from my eyes as I walked.

I took a deep breath and wiped away my tears then looked up to the sky and wondered what was I going to do now, I heard a familiar noise coming towards me, I turned, and Silver stopped in front of me he knew I was upset, he stood still and let me hug him. Most of the time Silver would manage to escape the fields and just wander about the stables and forest but he would always find his way back home to me.

I stayed with Silver for a while, being with him always made me feel better and this time I definitely needed him. I sat down on the ledge of the fountain nearby, Silver stayed close to me to make sure I was alright and there was someone else nearby who had been keeping an eye on me the entire time. He walked over to me and sat down beside me, he looked at me with his sad green eyes that sparkled in the sun.

Silver walked up to him and started to push his head up against him, Tristan lost his balance and nearly fell into the fountain.

"Whoa easy Silver, I don't want to get wet." He said and stroked Silver's nose. I laughed as Silver pushed Tristan more, it was a good thing Tristan was a strong shapeshifter as any normal boy would have already fell in. Silver finally got bored as he realized he could not win and headed off to the fields to eat more grass. We sat in silence as we watched him leave and then Tristan spoke.

"I contacted the other Mystical Knights and told them what happened, I understand if you want to stay here tonight. I can keep watch in my panther form outside, so I don't have to go into the house and disturb the others."

I looked at him and smiled, "Thank you but if it's alright with you I would rather go back to your house and keep training, Willow wanted us to get back to work, right."

"Yeah alright, you can stay with us for as long as you want." He smiled.

I nodded and looked back at Silver who was eating some long grass near the fence of one of the fields; I had to get stronger so I could protect him and everyone else I cared for. We heard footsteps approach us from behind; we turned around and saw Abbey.

"It's time; we can lay her to rest now. Are you ready?" She said.

I looked down at the jewel of darkness worried, it still felt heavy, and the colors kept changing from purple to red, then blue. I didn't want my magic to lose control around everyone. Tristan had noticed what I was looking at, he took my hand and said, "Come on Rose, don't worry I will stay with you."

Before I could reply he pulled me up to my feet and followed Abbey pulling me behind him.

Abbey led us to the small walled garden behind Unicorn Stables, I knew where we were going, it was a special garden where my mother was buried along with Willow's husband Charles, Willow would be laid to rest next to them. All the Unicorn members who lived there, were gathered around the garden with a few villagers who had managed to come too, I could see the minister with her son standing next to the vicar of the church who had come. They looked angry as they saw us approaching, Tristan saw Nick waving at us, so he headed towards him instead. Once we stopped next to Nick, Tristan let go of my hand and stepped back to give us some space.

Nick smiled at us both and asked, "Are you alright?"
I nodded and looked down at the ground, the grave was already dug, and her body wrapped up in silk had already been placed inside. I took a deep breath and stepped back a little, someone took hold of my hand, I looked up to see Helen, her eyes were red from crying too much, I squeezed her hand and she smiled at me. Beside her Hannah was holding her other hand and she was wiping her eyes with a tissue. Nick took hold of my other hand and the other Unicorn members held hands too. We were all together, I smiled knowing Willow would be happy, no matter what happens we were still a family and always will be.

We all looked at Anthony who had stepped forward and walked to the head of the grave; he took a deep breath then looked at us all.

"Before the vicar says a few words, I have a letter Willow wanted me to read to you all." He took another breath before he continued,

"To all my darling children who I have had the pleasure to help raise throughout my life. I would like to say thank you. Thank you for making my life complete, thank you for making me smile and laugh. You have all giving me such joy and love throughout these many long years and I am very proud of you all. I know you will be sad but try your best to smile and laugh together, stay strong and protect each other. I love you all so much and do not worry we will see each other again in another life, in another world. Now all of you go live the best you can, enjoy your life and get back to work."

Anthony then placed the letter back in his pocket, he was smiling but tears were falling from his eyes, Helen let go of my hand then walked over to him to give him a hug.
I heard weeping beside me it was Hannah, I knelt down beside her.
"Don't cry; remember Willow wanted us to keep smiling." I said.
"I.... I know but.....but it's hard I can't seem to stop."
I pulled her to me and gave her a hug, "Don't worry we will be alright." I said but I wasn't sure myself. I knew the others would be finding it difficult, Willow was more like a mother to them as she had adopted them at a younger age, even after my mother had passed away and I was taking into Willow's care, she had always been more of a friend to me or maybe like an aunt, as at first I didn't want to get close to anyone after losing my mother but in time I became closer to the family at Unicorn Stables thanks to Willow not giving up on me. We would all struggle to deal with her loss.
As the vicar said a few words about life, death, magic, and Gods, one by one we sprinkled some soil into her grave and said goodbye. Then the Unicorn members grabbed a shovel and started to fill in the hole while the villagers watched in silence. Once done I sadly looked down at the ground it looked bare and empty, there was only mud and bits of grass. I looked over at

the other graves and saw the wonderful flowers were in full bloom and I could see the bees and butterflies buzzing all around them reminding me of the fun summer days we had all spent together, even though the dead was sleeping underneath there were covered in life. I knew what Willow would like, a lot of flowers. I stepped forward and knelt, then I placed my hand on her grave I took a deep breath and concentrated, I could feel the earth and the roots all around me. I asked the jewel to lend me its power and it started to glow a bright green; I felt the magic within me stir.

"Rose, what are you doing?" Asked Tristan through our mind link.

I ignored him and continued; the flowers started to appear all around us. All different types sparkled in the sun; there covered Willow's grave and spread throughout the garden, the villagers gasped behind me. I smiled as I expanded my power to help more flowers grow. I felt a hand on my shoulder,

"That's enough Rose."

I looked up into the eyes of Odin, he must have come as soon as he had received Tristan's message. He looked sad but also worried as he pulled me to my feet.

"What kind of witchcraft is this?" Yelled Claudia behind the villagers. Everyone had stepped away from me and they looked scared, I looked at them confused, I had not done anything wrong, had I?

"What's wrong?" I asked Odin.

He looked into my eyes and smiled, "Nothing is wrong, you have helped the flowers grow and made this area look lovely. Anyone who sees differently are just simple minded. And I know Willow would be happy with this." He said loudly for everyone to hear, then he took hold of my hand and said, "Come on

Rose lets go somewhere to talk, you too Tristan."
Tristan growled he looked angrily at the villagers but
he followed us to a nearby bench in the garden far
enough away from the others so they would not hear
our conversation.

"I'm sorry to hear about Willow, she was a kind
woman, and the world will be a lot duller without her in
it, will you be alright?" Odin said.

I nodded I did not know what to say and I could see
the villagers making their way out of the garden with
fear in their eyes, were they really scared of me? I
thought.

"Do you want to stay here tonight?" He asked.

"No, I would rather go back with you, I need to learn
more about magic so I can become stronger, and I
need to make sure I can control the jewel, so it
doesn't lose control again." I replied.

Odin glanced at Tristan then nodded, "Alright if that's
what you want but don't push yourself too hard, you
have just used a lot of magic do you feel alright?"

"Yeah, I feel fine; I guess I'm getting used to it." I said
as I touched the jewel with my hand, I still felt tired,
but I didn't feel like I was going to pass out. Odin
smiled and put his hand on my shoulder,

"Good, we will help you the best we can."

"Thank you." I smiled.

We suddenly heard someone shouting, it was Jack
coming back through the gate, I had seen him leave
earlier with James, he ran past us on the bench and
stopped at Anthony and Helen who were walking
towards us.

"A delivery has come!" He shouted.

Hannah and Nick arrived from the other side of the
garden to see what all the fuss was about.

"That can't be right, we aren't expecting one and I
don't even know if we can afford one right now." Said

Helen. I stood up and walked over to them.

"No, it's alright, the delivery men said it had already been paid for by Willow last week, there are two carts full." Explained Jack after he had gotten his breath back. We all looked at each other confused, two carts full of horse food, bedding, our food and supplies would last us a long time, but it must have cost a fortune, how did Willow afford that?

"It looks like Willow is still looking after you all." Laughed Odin who had come up behind us with Tristan.

We all smiled, and Anthony said, "Right we better get to work and start unloading the carts, do you think you could help us?" He turned to Tristan and Odin.

"Of course, we would be happy to help." Said Odin. And Tristan nodded.

We all walked out of the garden together and headed back towards the front of the house where the carts were stood, the delivery men were waiting with James.

They had come from Crow Nest Village, a large market port three days ride away from us. Their village supplies all the other nearby villages with food, horse supplies and other equipment and gifts from around the world. The carts were full, how had Willow brought all of this, and did she know what was going to happen to her? I thought. I stood and stared at the carts as the others went over to look inside them, how are we going to manage without her?

Helen started talking to the delivery men while the others got to work unloading the carts but before I could start to help them I noticed Doctor Thomas walking into the house with Claudia, so I decided to follow them as I wanted to ask the doctor something, I wanted to find out more about Willow's illness.

"Where are you going Rose?" Shouted Nick from

behind me.

"I will be back in a minute." I yelled back and quickly walked towards the house before anyone could stop me.

I heard voices coming from the office, they must have gone in there, so I headed towards the door but before I entered I hesitated as I heard Claudia ask a question.

"Could magic users be the cause of Willow's death?"

"I admit it could have been a possibility, but I don't think that was the case for her, as she was on medication for a while because of her heart so I don't think magic had anything to do with it." Said the doctor.

"Yes but you yourself admitted that the events at the festival caused her heart to weaken, maybe she would still be alive if it wasn't for that." She said.

"Maybe, but it could have happened any time, any stressful situation could have caused it."

"Well, if you believe that doctor, that's fine but I still think magic is the cause of this, have you not heard the rumors about the jewel around Rose's neck. Some people are calling it the death necklace, that can't be a coincidence."

"I understand Claudia but there are just rumors, Rose is a good girl." He said.

"I know, I'm not blaming Rose but there has been nothing but trouble since she got that necklace, and I knew those damn magic users moving here would cause us problems and now one of our own is dead. I just know more danger is to come here, I just hope no one else from our village gets hurt."

"Well, we will just have to make sure everyone stays safe." Said Doctor Thomas.

"The only way that is going to happen is if all the magic users leave this village and they can take that necklace with them." Said Claudia.

The door then opened and out walked the doctor and Claudia, I quickly took a step back I didn't mean to eavesdrop, but I couldn't help it, was it really all my fault, was Willow dead because of me? I thought as tears welled up in my eyes.

Doctor Thomas saw me and dropped his bag to the ground, then he held his hand out to me, "Rose?" He said.

Before he could stop me I turned and ran, tears were falling from my eyes as the news sank in, it was all my fault. The jewel around my neck was heating up again and I could feel its power all around me, it turned black.

I ran out the back door and headed towards Dark Forest, I had to get away from here before I lost control. Silver had felt my distress, he ran in front of me and stopped then he bent his head down to let me climb on, he knew where I needed to go. Once I was on his back I held on tight, and he took off fast towards Dark Forest.

Chapter 15.
Danger in Dark Forest.

Silver ran fast and took me to waterfall cave, a secret place my mother had found long ago, it wasn't a large waterfall, but the lake and river could get deep when it rained, and the cave wasn't behind the waterfall but beside it. It also wasn't large, but it could fit a handful of people in it to shelter from the rain, which I had done a few times in the past. The trees and plants grew thick around here but there was always a gap at a certain point if you knew where to look so you could get to the clearing in front of the waterfall.

I jumped off Silver and entered the clearing between two trees, I glanced behind me and noticed Silver walking off back in the direction we had come, he knew I needed space. I fell to my knees and screamed; the magic exploded out of the jewel and darkened the grass, plants, and trees around me as though they had been burnt by fire.

I gasped as I felt pain in my left hand, it had also been burnt by the magic and I felt dizzy. I took a deep breath to try and calm down, the jewel went back to normal, and it felt lighter. I slowly stood up and headed towards the river the dizziness wore off; I knelt down and put my hand in the water to cool it. The skin was red and black, and it was sore, if only I could heal myself, I thought.

Lucas's reflection appeared in the water, "**You should never have come here alone, it's too dangerous.**" He said.

"Go away, I want to be alone. It's safer for everyone, you know that." I replied as I took my hand out of the water.

"**Rose, behind you!**"

I jumped up and spun around.

"You know you're going mad when you start talking to yourself." Laughed Caleb who appeared from behind the trees.

I took my dagger out of my belt and held it up in front of me; I was ready to defend myself.

He laughed again, "Now now, is that anyway to greet a friend."

"How did you find me?" I asked.

He looked at me puzzled, "Have the Mystical Knights taught you nothing, if you use dark magic it's easy for the Shadow Guild to find you."

"Dark magic?"

He pointed at the grass and trees around us, "Was it not you that killed these plants?"

"I…. I didn't mean to."

Caleb walked up to me and sat on a nearby log, I took a step back and kept my dagger pointed towards him.

"Dark magic isn't something you should fear Rose, it's something you should learn to control. Think of what you can do with that power if you join me, I can teach you."

"I don't want that power I don't want to hurt anyone." I said.

"Really? I heard you were practicing magic with the Mystical Knights."

"That is different it's good magic, light magic. I want to help people, not hurt them like you did." I said.

"Light and dark magic is basically one and the same, it's only a matter of perspective and I haven't hurt anyone, yet." He smirked.

"You've got to be kidding me; Willow is dead because of you!" I shouted.

He looked at me confused, "I am sorry about that, but it wasn't me, I didn't order my pets to kill anyone, I just wanted to see what you could do with the jewel."

"She had a weak heart and because she had to run from the shadow demons she got worse and now she's dead, it's your fault! Maybe I should rip out your heart!" I yelled with anger.

Caleb laughed then stood up and faced me, "Careful Rose, you're starting to sound like one of us."

"Shut up!" I shouted and magic flew from my dagger and headed towards Caleb, he jumped out of the way just in time. I looked down at the jewel it had turned black again; my anger was causing it to lose control.

"Rose please calm down; I truly am sorry about your friend. Think about what I can offer you if you join us, we can teach you how to control your anger and the dark magic inside of you, so you won't hurt anyone. I will leave you alone to think about it, but I warn you, I'm not a patient man."

I took a deep breath and lowered my weapon.

"You don't have to wait; my answer will still be no." I replied.

"Really, then why did you hesitate? Look around you, look at the damage you can cause, look at your hand. We can help you; I will leave you to think it over but while you do I will let you train with my pets, it's the best way for you to learn." He smiled and clicked his fingers together, shadow demons appeared from the ground they were shaped like men and were carrying swords.

The first shadow lunged at me and swung its sword, I blocked its attack with ease remembering my training with Tristan. I then fired a bolt of magic through my dagger, it hit the demon and it vanished with a scream.

Caleb laughed "Well done Rose."

Then he disappeared into darkness, the other three demons screamed out a war cry and charged at me all together. I jumped out of the way and defended myself with my dagger; it was difficult because their swords were heavier and longer than my dagger so they could reach me sooner. A sword scratched my arm, and I hissed in pain, I sent off another wave of magic and it destroyed two demons but that only made the third one angry, it screamed again. My ears burned with pain and the ground rumbled as more shadows appeared to fight.

I gripped my dagger tighter and waited for the next attack, but I wasn't prepared for what happened next, a different shadow appeared in front of me, and it lunged. It was a lot bigger than the others but that was not the problem, the problem was during the fight with the others I had stepped too close to the water's edge. So when the shadow demon jumped on me we both tumbled into the deep lake.

Deep water is my weakness as I can't swim, at six years old I had jumped into a river to save a friend's kitten and if my mother hadn't jumped in to save me I would have died that day. She saved me and the kitten just in time. My mother had asked Nick's father to teach me after that but every time I got close to deep water I had a panic attack and froze with fear so my mother decided it would be best to try again when I got older, but I never did, I've been staying away from deep water ever since.

Now I was in trouble, the shadow was pulling me deeper into the lake, I felt myself getting weaker, my chest was tight as I tried to hold my breath. My heart was pounding, and darkness was surrounding me, I wasn't sure if it was the shadow causing it or because I was close to passing out.

There was nothing I could do even my magic couldn't help me; I couldn't call for help and even if I could, no one would hear me but then I remembered there was someone who could hear me, and I didn't even have

to make a sound. I called his name in my mind,
"Tristan."
A hand grabbed my arm and pulled me back to the
surface, I started to cough up the water and I blinked
in surprise, it was not Tristan beside me it was Nick.
He helped me get back on dry land and stood close to
me as I knelt and tried to get my breath back. I looked
up and noticed Nick was not alone, Tristan was in his
panther form and Odin was there too and they were
both fighting off the last shadow demons.
"Are you alright Rose?" Asked Nick with concern.
I was breathing heavily, and I was shaking but I was
still alive so I nodded at him, but then I suddenly
remembered the large shadow that pulled me into the
water it was still here, and I could sense it
approaching us.
I jumped to my feet and yelled, "Nick, watch out!"
Then I pushed him out of the way.
At that moment, the large shadow emerged out of the
water and changed its form into a wolf as it lunged at
me. I heard a loud roar behind me, and a black
panther jumped and collided with the shadow wolf
before it could touch me.
The shadow wolf disappeared, and Odin walked over
to us, "I think that was the last one, is everyone
alright?" He said.
Nick and I both nodded, Tristan walked past us
growling and stopped near Odin's horse there was a
flash of light as he turned back into his human form.
Silver was stood there too, and I wondered if he had
led the others to me.
"Rose?" Said Odin as he looked at me with concern.
"I'm alright thank you." I replied.
"Yeah that was close." Said Nick as he pushed
himself up off the floor and smiled at me.
Tristan came back towards us from the horses he was

now wearing a pair of tracksuit trousers and wrapped in a cloak he must have gotten out of the saddle bag. Even though he was human again it was the angriest I had ever seen him, and he was heading straight for me, he grabbed hold of the front of my top with both hands and yelled,

"What the hell were you thinking, why would you come here alone? You stupid idiot you could have been killed!"

"Hey, let go of her!" Shouted Nick.

Tristan took a deep breath then let go of me and took a step back he had noticed the tears in my eyes.

"I…. I'm sorry I wanted to be alone, look around you I'm dangerous, I didn't want to hurt anyone else."

"What do you mean? Rose you haven't hurt anyone." Said Odin.

"Willow is dead because of me, it's my fault, you all know it's true." The tears started to fall from my eyes.

"Rose it is not your fault, she didn't die because of magic she was ill." Said Odin.

"The shadows chased her and caused her heart pain, and the shadows were there because of me, I put everyone in danger it's better if I stay alone, no one should die for me." I said quietly.

Odin pulled me to him and gave me a hug,

"Well tough, were not going anywhere, Willow knew you would blame yourself that's why she wrote me that letter telling me to keep you close and safe and to stand by you know matter what, because you've blamed yourself before and tried to push people away, she didn't want you going through that again, she doesn't want you to be alone. I am here now to tell you; you are not alone, the Unicorn members are your family, and the Mystical Knights are your friends, we will all help you the best we can, and we will keep you safe."

The Magical Jewel, A Mystical Knight Novel, Book 1.
By Jade Stephenson ©.

I held Odin tighter and cried.
"Don't worry, you're not alone and you never will be."
He said.

Chapter 16.
History Lesson.

"It's a shame you didn't join us Rose, we could have had so much fun together." Said Finn who was smiling in front of me.

"Leave me alone!" I shouted.

Then I woke up. All night I had kept waking up because of nightmares. Once I had accidentally opened up my mind link with Tristan and screamed, he jumped into my room wearing nothing but shorts and holding his sword. After I had told him I was fine he went back to bed mumbling under his breath and rubbing his eyes.

I was still tired, and it was still early in the morning, but I could no longer sleep so I got out of bed, changed into my blue dress, and put on my black boots then wrapped my cloak around me. I grabbed my small mirror and made sure my dagger was tucked into my belt before heading downstairs to Odin's office, I knew what I needed to do.

I grabbed the book on the jewel of darkness off Odin's desk and headed outside to read, I knew I needed to finally learn more about the jewel, so I had a better chance to control it and use the magic within to help and protect the people and animals I care for.

I sat on the grass near the yard where the new stables would be built, I made sure I stayed closer to the house as I still felt nervous because of what had happened the day before and I did not want to worry the Mystical Knights.

I opened the large old book and started reading the first page, it read:

'The jewel of darkness was first researched by myself Nero Wolf. I am a scientist and researcher of magical items. My best friend a man named Jonah Walt was the first known person to carry the jewel of darkness. After realizing it held a lot of power, I decided to learn all I could about the jewel.

However, as I examined the jewel further there was an unfortunate accident, and my friend Jonah Walt was killed.

I also noticed the jewel had disappeared that same day and it was not seen again until the next year, I had heard a rumor of another magical jewel, so I went to investigate further but to my surprise it was the same jewel my friend had carried.

The second one to carry it was a woman named Anne Carter, but she was also killed by the magic within it. I then discovered the jewel would disappear every time the person carrying it would die then reappear again a year later with someone else. That is when I came up with the name jewel of darkness as anyone carrying it would die because of the magic stored within it.

After discovering other magical items and knowing others would wear the jewel of darkness but die because they could not control the magic within, I knew I needed to get help on this matter, I also understood the magical items and the ones who carry them needed to be protected. So, I went to an old friend for help, a shapeshifter king.

King Lionel Hart decided part of his royal knights would form a new team. That team would find and protect the magical items and be responsible for the ones who carry them, they would help train them and keep them safe. The team was named the Mystical Knights, also if the magic inside the items was too strong for the ones carrying them or if they were used to carry out evil deeds and hurt others, the magical items would be taken from them and stored in a safe room at the king's castle in Sunlight City.

The jewel of darkness is an item that cannot be taken from its owner as it somehow connects to them like a binding contract and only that *person can use it.*

On one of my many adventures I found an old stone tablet with a picture of a dragon and underneath it was the same shape as the jewel of darkness, by studying the tablet further I discovered the dragon king held power the same as the jewel and with that power he saved the land and his kind from darkness a long time ago. I believe the jewel is somehow connected to the dragons and it may even contain the soul of the last dragon king, but I have yet to prove this is true.'

I took the jewel from around my neck, held it in my hands and looked at it closely, a soul of a dragon, that is crazy, I thought.

Dragons flew through the skies many years ago; they lived in the forests, in caves and on top of mountains. Some even lived at the bottom of the oceans but some men started to hunt or control the dragons as it was known they were full of pure and strong magic, because of this, one by one, the dragons disappeared.

Some say they were all killed but some believe they are still alive today and are hiding, waiting for a day they can return and fly free in the skies once more. Many people have claimed to have seen a dragon, but these rumors were never proved true. When I was little I also claimed I had seen one flying in the sky above my head while I was sat in the garden at Unicorn Stables, but it was such a long time ago I can't remember if it was one or not. It was probably just a large bird.

I looked down at the mirror in front of me, "Hey Lucas, have you got a dragon in there with you?" I asked him.

He appeared and laughed, "**I don't think so, but the jewel has always felt alive to me, have you noticed that too?**"

"Yes, now that you mention it, it has always felt warm

as though it is alive, but a dragon's soul is that even possible?"
"Anything is possible I'm inside the jewel so why not a dragon king."
"I guess it would explain all the weird magic I can use." I smiled.
"Yes it would but there is magic all around us, close your eyes and clear your mind, you will be able to feel it and breathe it in like the air, it will help you control your magic better and strengthen your core. You will get used to using magic like I did."
I nodded and placed the jewel back around my neck, then I did what he had told me, I took a deep breath and closed my eyes I listened to the sounds all around me and felt the warm sun on my face, but Lucas was right I could feel something different, something strong. It felt like raindrops hitting my skin, but it was magic, I could feel it surrounding my entire body, I wasn't scared, I felt free and happy.
I let my senses travel further and let more magic seep inside my body; I could feel the earth all around me it was filled with nature and life.
There were roots under the ground in front of me, roots of a tree struggling to grow so I let my magic pour over them and helped them come to life. I could sense it growing in front of me and I smiled as more magic washed over the tree, I felt it grow bigger and the roots thickened. I was being watched, I could feel three heartbeats behind me, but I didn't stop I knew one heart belonged to Tristan as I could sense his mind link. I opened my eyes and witnessed the tree grow tall; it became a large willow tree. I took another deep breath and stopped my magic; the jewel cooled down and stopped glowing a bright green.
I turned around and saw Odin, Tristan and Marigold

standing behind me and they looked shocked.
Marigold even looked scared, so I quickly jumped to
my feet, but I lost my balance and had to be caught
by Odin and Tristan.
"Whoa, careful Rose." Said Odin.
"I'm sorry I didn't mean to.... I just wanted to practice
a little, I know using my magic is bad, I.....I'm sorry." I
said as I pushed away from them.
I moved closer to the tree I had just helped grow, it
sparkled in the morning sun.
"You have no reason to apologize I am glad you are
learning how to control your magic. This magic......
No, your magic, it is beautiful." Odin smiled at me
then looked at the tree, I also smiled.
"Next time though, don't use your magic when you are
alone, remember we are here to help you." Odin said.
"Thank you, I know but I wasn't alone, Lucas was with
me." I smiled down at the mirror that was still on the
ground, and I could see Lucas smiling up at me and
he had his two thumbs up in the air.
Suddenly Marigold shouted, "This is crazy!"
We all looked at her and I said, "I'm not lying I really
can see him."
"No that's not what I mean, come on, I can't be the
only one that's shocked only the fairy queen can do
this. How can you have this power?" She said and
pointed at the tree.
I shrugged my shoulders and looked back at the tree,
was it really bad to help this tree grow, I thought.
"Wait, I thought you can help plants grow too." I
looked back at Marigold.
"Yes, all fairies can help certain plants grow and the
strongest of us can grow larger plants but only the
fairy queen can grow trees, in fact when it is time to
choose who will be next in line for the throne only the
one with this power can rule next. If the other fairies

hear about this they might consider you a threat to their kingdom." She said.

"Oh…. I'm sorry I didn't mean to offend you or the fairies but it's not dangerous magic so how can I be a threat to them?" I asked confused.

"It's complicated." She said.

"It's nothing for you to worry about Rose, and Marigold we are yet to discover the full power the jewel has, it could contain all the magic of every species and I'm positive you can handle it Rose. We will all learn about it together." Said Odin but even he sounded worried.

I looked towards Tristan who had stayed quiet, he was looking down at the mirror I had left on the ground, and he looked sad he probably wished he could see his brother too. I picked the mirror back up and put it back inside my pocket then I sat back down on the grass and started to flick through the pages of the book.

"Well, come back to the house when you are ready but please don't use any more magic today I don't want you to overdo it." Said Odin.

I nodded and he walked off back towards the house with Marigold, Tristan sat down next to me.

I was trying to read but my mind was still full of grief and confusion, and I was tired. Also reading about how others have died wearing the same jewel that was now around my neck was not helping me at all.

I slammed the book shut and rubbed my head, "This isn't helping." I said out loud.

Tristan smiled at me and said, "Yeah it's not a very good book and the ending is rubbish."

"Yes and book two doesn't sound like it's going to be any better." I laughed.

I looked up at the tree I helped grow, it is strange that it would be a willow tree I helped after Willow died. I wondered how the others were coping at Unicorn Stables.

Tristan stood up then held out his hand, "Come on Rose let's go and train some more with our swords, I think that will help you."

I smiled and took his hand, and he pulled me up to my feet, "You are right, beating you will help." We both laughed and walked back towards the house.

After we both had grabbed our wooden swords he started to teach me how to defend myself against certain attacks. We trained for a while and Odin gave us both good advice, Tristan was right it did help me, learning how to wield a sword took my mind off my problems and my grief.

After a while we heard horses running down the track towards us, we looked and spotted Nick on his horse Murphy and Silver was behind him, he must have been wandering around the forest again. Silver saw me and picked up his pace, he got to us first and he rubbed his head against me in greeting, I laughed "Hello boy."

Nick jumped off his horse and held his arms out towards Tristan.

"Hello, where is my hug?" He said.

Tristan backed away from him and Odin laughed, "Hello Nick, how are you and the others coping at Unicorn Stables?" Odin asked.

"Well, we are keeping things running, Helen and Hannah are finding things difficult but I'm sure we will all be fine in time." He replied then glanced at me. I smiled at him and continued to stroke Silver's nose.

"I came to let you know the supplies are ready for your new stables, but Noah wants us to meet him in the village and ride with him through the forest, after the events at the festival no one wants to travel alone anymore." Said Nick.

"We understand, why don't you three go and take Edmund and Marigold with you; I will stay here and make sure everything is ready for your return." Said Odin.

After Tristan, Marigold and Edmund had tacked their horses up we were ready to ride out, Silver wasn't wearing any tack today, but it was alright as he would let me ride him anyway and he knew where we were going. I gently put my riding gloves on to help protect my hand, Odin had bandaged my hand last night and it was still sore. We all mounted our horses then set off through the forest at a steady pace and in silence as we listened out for any sign of trouble, nothing happened but I could sense something. I had a bad feeling we were being watched.

Chapter 17.
Trouble Brewing.

We finally left Dark Forest and entered the village, I breathed a sigh of relief, we had made it. I thought I had sensed something in the forest, but Tristan and the horses hadn't looked scared so maybe it was just my imagination.

I turned around and looked at the tall trees, but I couldn't see anyone there, I heard a voice in my mind.

"**Rose, what's wrong?**" Asked Tristan.

"**Nothing.**" I replied and smiled.

We all dismounted our horses and led them through the village, Silver followed me like always. I noticed the change to the village straight away, instead of the happy villagers talking, laughing, and working together the place was quiet, no children were playing today. The villagers we did see, were sad and looked angry when they spotted us. The village was also a mess there were broken fences and windows and stone had also fell from some buildings, but the worst damage was to the Horse house, the building I had destroyed with my magic. The others had noticed the sad look on my face.

"Rose none of this is your fault." Said Marigold as we left our horses in the stalls so they could rest.

"Maybe not all of it." I replied as I looked again at the Horse house.

"Don't worry about it, that's nothing, you should see some of the mess I've caused with my magic." Laughed Edmund.

"Why am I not surprised." Said Nick.

We all laughed as we headed towards Noah's house. As we passed the village hall I noticed Claudia and Harry at the notice board where jobs, events and wanted posters were hung up, Harry was pinning something up on the board.

"I'm just going off to check something." I told the others and headed off in the direction of the village hall.

I stopped in front of the notice board as Harry and Claudia left and I read down the list of names they had pinned to the board, it was the riding event results but when I got to my name it had been crossed out and there was a note beside it saying, 'Disqualified No Magic Users Allowed.'

"What!" Shouted Nick who had come up behind me with the others and also read the list.

He then ran towards Claudia and Harry, who were standing near the fountain watching us, we followed him.

"Why has Rose been disqualified?" He shouted at them.

"There is no need to shout, as it says on the board no magic users are allowed to compete, some people believe you make yourself ride better using magic. You know the rules." Smiled Claudia.

"That's a lie." I shouted angrily and the jewel turned black.

"Really? You are becoming dangerous; we heard it was you who destroyed the Horse house." Smirked Harry and he pointed at the jewel.

"I…. That was an accident." I said quietly.

Claudia gasped and stepped away from us.

Tristan stood in front of me and growled in Harry's face, "I can show you dangerous if that's what you want."

Nick put his hand on Tristan's shoulder and said, "We better go, Noah is waiting."

Tristan nodded and we turned to walk away, as we followed Nick I heard Edmund say, "Damn I wanted to see a panther eat his meal today."

Claudia and Harry hurried off back home looking worried, Edmund winked at me, and I smiled back. We spotted Noah outside his house standing next to his cart filled with the supplies for the new stables, he was tying rope around the cart to hold everything in place and his apprentices David and Peter were helping him.

"Ah good you are here; we have just finished loading the cart." Said Noah when he spotted us. Nick shook Noah's hand in greeting, then Noah turned to me and gave me a hug.

"How are you Rose?" He asked.

"Hello, I'm alright thank you." I replied and pulled away from him.

Noah glanced at Nick, and he shrugged, they both knew I was lying.

"Well, I will just double check we have everything, then we can leave, Peter and David will be coming to help too." Said Noah and he pointed to the men.

They both waved at us, but they didn't look too happy about coming with us, in fact they kept glancing at me, and Tristan and they both looked scared. They have known me since I was little, were they really scared of me now that I can use magic, I thought as I looked at them.

Once Noah was ready we walked back through the village to get our horses, Noah's two large white horses, Buddy and Duke were pulling the cart with ease despite the heavy load they were both strong horses and they would get some apples for a treat once we arrived back at Old House.

As we walked through the village we noticed more people clearing up the mess and fixing some of the fences, they looked scared and mad as we walked past them. Some of the villagers started to whisper to each other,

"Magic users don't belong here, when are they leaving?"

"They are too dangerous to have near us, my children are scared."

"They even have Rose using magic now, what would her mother think?"

"That boy can change into a panther; he could attack us."

I clenched my fists in anger; the Mystical Knights had helped them, why would they say such things.

We got back to our horses, and I climbed back onto Silver, he sensed I was upset so he started to trot towards the forest.

"Whoa boy it's alright; we should wait for the others." I told him.

As we started the journey back through the forest Tristan had noticed I had slowed down and was behind, so he turned Patrick around and walked him beside Silver.

"How do you stay calm when people say mean things about you and your friends?" I asked him.

"I forgot you have good ears too, sometimes I don't stay calm but that only makes things worse. I try to remember it's not always their fault most people only say mean things out of fear or anger, and some people have only heard the bad stories about magic, so they just assume were all bad. They don't know any better and I guess I've grown used to it." He said.

"Oh right." I said quietly. And I wondered will the villagers act like that around me from now on.

"Rose, you can't let what they say get to you. Ignore them; show them how kind and strong you can be." Said Tristan in my mind.

"Alright, thank you Tristan." I replied through our mind link and smiled.

He nodded and we hurried our horses on to catch up with the others.

As we all ventured further into the forest a pheasant flew out of a bush and spooked the horses but luckily they calmed down once they realized it was just a bird, so we carried on. David and Peter looked nervous, and they kept tight hold of their daggers expecting a fight.

On the ride back to Old House we all stayed alert and quiet, even though nothing happened, something did not feel right.

It was like the calm before the storm.

Chapter 18.
Shadows closing in.

One stable was already completed so I was sat under the shade of the willow tree I had helped grow, having a rest and drinking some juice with Odin and Marigold while Noah, Peter, David, Edmund, Tristan, and Nick started work on building the second stable. It hadn't been too difficult to build as Noah had made the pieces of wood and metal fit together well, so we just had to line the pieces up and fit them together, Noah had also said my designs helped with the instructions but the main reason we were getting the job done quickly, was because we were all working well as a team.

Even Peter and David had started to talk more with the Mystical Knights and no longer looked scared, they were both interested in knowing what living at Sunlight City was like. I could hear them all laughing at another funny story Edmund was telling them. I smiled and took another sip of my drink, the day had become warmer, but it did feel like rain was on its way, hopefully we would be finished before it started.

"Oh, looks like I need some more tea, I will go and get some more drinks for everyone." Said Odin as he got up and stretched his legs.

"I can help." I said and got up to follow him.

"Thank you Rose." He smiled.

We both carried a tray of cups and glasses back to the house, as we walked I asked, "Odin where is Isabella and Clover?"

"They were going to the village to buy some paint so they can decorate Clover's room, didn't you see them on the way back here?" He replied looking confused.

"No, we didn't see anyone on the way back."

"Well maybe they're still in the house." Said Odin but he looked worried.
We walked into the kitchen and put the trays down on the table, Odin got some more cups and glasses out of the cupboard.
"I will go and see if they are upstairs." I said and walked back out the door.

I started to walk up the stairs, but I didn't get very far as a shadow demon jumped down the steps and collided into me and we both tumbled down the stairs and landed in a heap on the floor. I tried to get up fast, but the shadow pinned me to the floor and howled in my face, it looked like a wolf, and it used its teeth to rip the bandage off my arm and dug its claws into the wound that had already scabbed over, the wound reopened.
"Get off me!" I shouted and kicked with all my strength.
The shadow demon jumped off me and spat something out of its mouth, it was an envelope, before I could attack the demon, it jumped through the window shattering the glass with a loud bang.
"Rose are you alright!" Shouted Odin as he ran out of the kitchen.
"Yeah, I think so." I replied and glanced down at my arm.
 He spotted the blood running down my arm and he looked angry, he ran to the broken window and looked out, but the shadow had gone.
I bent down and picked up the envelope the shadow had dropped, it was addressed to me, so I opened it up and read the note inside, Odin watched me.
I went cold and my heart skipped a beat as I read the words but before I could show Odin the message, Tristan ran into the house, quickly followed by the

others.

Odin nodded at them, "We are alright, Rose what does the letter say?"

Instead of answering him I handed him the letter then sat down on the bottom step of the staircase.

"If you want your friends back unharmed and alive follow the demon through the forest to find me and exchange them for the jewel. Finn." Odin read the letter out loud so everyone could hear.

"Damn it!" Shouted Edmund.

"Wait who does he have?" Asked Marigold.

"I'm sorry I think he has taken Clover and Isabella." Answered Odin.

"No!" Cried Marigold and tears appeared in her eyes.

Nick put a hand on her shoulder and asked, "What should we do?"

"It's obvious, we need to follow the demon, find Finn, kill him then get the girls back." Shouted Edmund.

"Um hasn't the demon already left?" I asked quietly and pointed to the broken window.

Everyone looked around the entrance hall then quickly ran out of the house; I got up and followed them.

"Over there!" Yelled Noah who had spotted it first.

We looked in the direction he was pointing and saw the shadow demon standing near the forest, its red eyes were watching us, and it was waiting.

Before anyone else could say anything, a horse suddenly appeared out of the forest with two riders on its back, it galloped past the demon and came down the track, luckily the shadow did not move. It was Anthony and Helen riding Sam they stopped at the gate and dismounted; they saw us near the house, so they ran towards us.

"We need your help!" Yelled Anthony.

"Whoa, easy Anthony, what's wrong?" Asked Nick. Anthony took a deep breath and looked at me, "We need your jewel." He said.

"Why?" I asked but I had a bad feeling I already knew the answer. Helen took out a note from her pocket and gave it to me.

"They have taken Hannah, James and Jack." She said and I saw tears in her eyes.

I read the note: 'If you want your friends back unharmed and alive go to Rose, I will exchange them for the jewel. Finn.'

I looked towards Nick and nodded then I handed the note back to Helen and started walking towards the forest, but Odin stopped me, he grabbed my uninjured arm and shouted,

"And where the hell do you think you're going?"

I pointed towards the demon, "They've taken our friends, my family, so I'm going to do what our letter said, I'm going to follow the demon and bring everyone back, so are you coming?"

"Don't be stupid, I'm a Mystical Knight of course I'm going but you are not." Odin replied.

"What! I am not staying here, and in case you've forgotten I'm the only one who can carry the jewel." I shouted back.

"As Mystical Knights our number one priority is to protect the magical items and the ones who carry them and make sure the items don't fall into the wrong hands, so you are staying here." Said Odin.

"But…." Before I could argue further I was interrupted.

"I suggest we come up with a plan." Said Tristan.

"Right. Noah, Peter, and David, I think you three should go back to the village, thank you for all your help today." Said Odin.

"Are you sure you won't need our help?" Asked Noah

with concern.

"No, I will not let anyone else become involved in this, it's too dangerous, the best thing you can do is go home and make sure the village is safe." Said Odin.

"Well alright but please be careful." Said Noah and he left with Peter and David to get their horses ready to go home, the men looked relieved they were not following the demon.

The Mystical Knights came up with a plan; Helen was to pretend she was me as she was the right height and for some reason Odin was not letting Marigold go with them. Helen would distract Finn and the demons with Tristan by her side while Odin, Edmund and Anthony would rescue the others. It was a good plan, but they still wouldn't let me go with them, and Marigold and Nick were staying behind too. I argued for a while that I should go, and I didn't like Helen taking my place as bait, but Odin and the others knew it would be best if I stayed, Odin said he didn't want to risk me losing control of my magic when they were trying to save the others, so in the end I agreed with the plan and Tristan bandaged up my arm.

As Odin and Edmund got their horses ready to leave I noticed Marigold having a heated conversation with them both, she also was not happy about being left behind, it was her sister they had taken after all. I heard Odin telling Marigold he would find it difficult to explain to the fairy Queen he had lost two members of her tribe, so that is why he insisted Marigold was to stay behind, to protect me and Nick. And if the plan were to fail, Marigold would have to take us to Sunlight City so the other Mystical Knights could protect us and keep the jewel safe.

I didn't tell Odin this, but I would not leave if the plan

were to fail, I would not run away from the fight, I would not leave my home, family, and friends in the hands of a mad man who would do anything to get what he wants, and I would not let the dark guild win. I, Marigold, and Nick watched the others leave, the shadow demon saw them approaching so it took off to lead them through the forest, the horses and Tristan in his panther form followed close behind.

Before Tristan vanished out of sight I opened up our mind link and said,
"Please be careful."
"Don't worry, we will all come home soon." He replied and disappeared into the trees.
I saw Marigold wipe the tears from her eyes, so I took hold of her hand and said,
"Don't worry, they will be alright." but I wasn't too sure. We stood there for a while, and we waited.

Chapter 19.
Seeing Double.

Darkness covered the land and the moon rose in the sky, the stars twinkled once the rain had stopped and the clouds cleared, the air smelt damp and it had turned cooler, but we still waited.

No one had returned and Marigold had made herself busy by clearing up the glass of the broken window, Nick boarded up the window with some wood and I had fed the horses. After we had done that, we stood on the track once more and waited again for any sign of the others coming back. I squeezed the pommel of the sword in my belt that I had taken from Odin's office, Marigold had insisted we should arm ourselves with weapons just in case any more shadow demons were to appear.

I turned towards Nick and Marigold, who were stood behind me and said,

"I think we have waited long enough; I think it's time we go and look for them."

Nick shrugged his shoulders and looked towards Marigold, she took a deep breath and replied,

"No, we should wait a bit longer."

Before I could argue with her, Nick shouted, "Look!" And he pointed towards the forest, but it wasn't our family and friends who appeared out of the trees it was another shadow demon and like the last one that had appeared it was also shaped like a wolf, and it was running at full speed towards us.

We took our swords out of our belts and stood ready for a fight, but the shadow wolf stopped in front of us and dropped a letter from its mouth, then sat down, it stared at us with its glowing red eyes.

I slowly walked towards it and picked up the letter,

Nick pointed his sword at the shadow demon while I read the letter out loud.

"The rescue mission was a nice try but it failed, and now I have more of your friends, if you want them all back bring the jewel to me, follow my pet to find me and please no more games I am running out of patience, and I would hate it if anyone were to get hurt. Caleb."

I threw the letter on the ground, and I felt the jewel heat up as I became angry.

"Well now we definitely have to go!" I shouted.

"We can't." Marigold said quietly.

"What!" I yelled.

"Calm down Rose, we need to think of a plan first." Said Nick.

"No, Odin said if anything were to happen to them, we were to leave and go to Sunlight City." Explained Marigold as she picked the letter up off the ground and put it in her pocket.

"Are you crazy, we can't leave now; we have to save the others and you can't leave your sister." I said.

Marigold turned to me with anger and tears in her eyes, "Do you think this is easy for me, we don't have a choice if the Dark Shadow Guild were to get the jewel of darkness the whole world will be in danger, as Mystical Knights we would sacrifice our lives to make sure that doesn't happen, they all knew that when they left."

"He hasn't just taken Mystical Knights, my family didn't ask to be involved in any of this, they hate magic users; I would never forgive myself if they were to die because of me."

Nick put a hand on my shoulder and said, "Look, I know this is hard but maybe Marigold is right, I also don't think the Unicorn members would want the Dark Shadow Guild to get hold of the jewel of darkness, and anyway what can we do, they have already caught the strongest fighters and we know we can't give them the jewel and it's not like we have another one to give them instead, so our best choice is to leave and find others that can help us."

Marigold nodded but something Nick said had given me an idea and I knew who to ask for help, I took the small mirror from my belt pouch and spoke to it.

"Lucas I need your help; do you remember when you read the book on the jewel, there was a story about a woman, I think she was an explorer. She could use a magic no one else could with the jewel, do you think I could use that same magic now on the jewel?"

Lucas's eyes lit up a bright green as he realized what I was planning, and he smiled. **"Your ideas are crazier than mine, but it could work, Caleb would be distracted long enough for Marigold and Nick to rescue the others**."

"No, Rose you can't be seriously thinking about using that magic!" Said Marigold with concern.

"Can someone please fill me in, what are you talking about and what magic?" Said Nick who looked confused.

"In the book on the jewel of darkness there is a story of a woman, an explorer named Lara Drake who could use the jewel well, in fact she had the jewel longer than anyone and she had a unique power only she could use. She could make copies of objects, clone them and there would look identical. She called it spell of clone; I think Rose wants to use that magic now on the jewel." Marigold explained.

"Ah, I see." Said Nick.

"It's risky though, no one else has been able to do it and I don't think even Lara could copy the jewel, it's unique it may not work."

I looked down at Lucas, he smiled and gave me a thumbs up.

"Lucas believes I can do it, so I'm going to try." I said.

"He's even crazier than you are, Tristan would be proud. Wait! What about your mind link with him, could you not communicate with him so he can let us know how they are doing?" Said Marigold.

I slammed the palm of my hand against my forehead, I had not thought about that.

"Tristan, can you hear me? Are you alright?" I asked him through our mind link but there was no answer.

"He's not answering maybe we are too far away." I told them.

"Or he's choosing to ignore you because he doesn't want us to worry." Said Nick.

There was another reason, but I didn't want to think about that right now hopefully they were all safe for the moment; I took the jewel from around my neck.

"Well, I think it's time we start our plan." I said.

"Wait Rose, I think you should try copying something else first before the jewel, this should be alright." Said Marigold and she handed me her dagger. I nodded and looked at the mirror in my hand

"Any tips on how to do this?" I asked.

"Just believe you can do it and concentrate, clear your mind, and picture the dagger then imagine you can see two. The jewel should do the rest, I know you can do it, you are strong." Smiled Lucas.

"Thanks, alright I will try my best." I handed Nick my mirror then I knelt as though I was praying and held out both my hands with my palms facing up, the dagger and jewel was in one hand and my other hand was empty. I don't know why I chose to be in this position, but something told me it was the right thing to do, it was like my instincts knew how to do the spell of clone as though the jewel controlled my movements.

I closed my eyes and took a deep breath; I could feel the dagger Marigold had given me and I tried to picture another one in my other hand. I willed the jewel to make a copy and I concentrated hard, I felt the jewel heat up and the magic was swarming around me.

"Whoa!!" Said Nick and I heard Marigold gasp.

I opened my eyes and saw a second dagger had appeared in my other hand and it looked identical to the other one.

"Wow, you did it Rose, are you feeling alright?" Asked Marigold.

"I'm fine." I lied as I was feeling weak.

I slowly stood up and handed both daggers to Nick, he looked at them closely.

"They look the same, but I think the one you made feels lighter." He said.

"That's alright it shouldn't matter with the jewel as Caleb has never held it before, so he wouldn't know how it feels." Said Marigold.

"So, are you ready to try it on the jewel?" Said Nick, then he glanced at the shadow wolf that had sat quietly and waited the entire time.

I nodded and knelt down again, I did the same as before but this time I kept my eyes open so I could see the jewel and picture another one. As my magic started to work, the jewel lifted into the air and glowed a bright blue color, it was a lot harder than before, and it took longer but another jewel finally appeared, and it floated next to the original.

I fell to one side exhausted, luckily Nick was there to catch me, both jewels floated down towards me, so I caught them both and checked them, they both looked the same.

"Rose are you alright? And don't lie to us this time."
Said Nick.

I smiled at him, "I'm just tired that was harder than I
thought it would be."

"Did it work; do the jewels look the same?" Asked
Marigold.

"Yes, there both look the same, but I can't sense any
magic from the fake one and it's cold." I replied.

"I did say the jewel was unique I had a feeling the
magic wouldn't transfer over to the fake one, but
that's better for us we don't want Caleb getting his
hands on any of your magic and becoming stronger,
I'm sure he won't notice." Said Marigold.

I put the fake jewel around my neck and put the real
one into the inside pocket of my cloak, then I carefully
got to my feet with the help of Nick.

"Are you sure you can manage this Rose, maybe you
should rest first." Said Marigold.

"No, I will be fine don't worry; it's time to go we have
kept Caleb waiting long enough."

"Alright but if you need to rest on the way please let
us know and remember you have to drop some of
your blood onto the fake jewel so Caleb thinks your
transferring the jewel to him so he thinks he can use
it."

"Right." I replied.

We got our horses out of the field ready to ride into
the forest, we decided not to put tack on them so they
could escape easily if they needed to and as Murphy
followed Silver everywhere, we knew they would find
their way back home. Marigold also knew she could
easily find her mare Blue again if she got lost so she
was not worried.

We set off walking towards the shadow wolf, it saw us
coming so it got up to lead us through the forest.
Marigold smiled, "Alright lets teach this Dark Shadow

Guild not to mess with us."
"Yeah, they're in trouble now." Laughed Nick beside us but we all looked worried.
We entered the forest, following the shadow demon one step at a time.

Chapter 20.
The Rescue.

The journey through Dark Forest following the
shadow demon wolf was tough, we jumped at every
little sound or movement which did not help my
nerves. It was also hard to see where we were going
in the dark but luckily the jewel was giving us some
light. And after a while we had to get off our horses as
the path was no longer suitable to ride on. I was
already tired from using too much magic, but we had
to climb over tree roots and go through bushes to get
to where the others were waiting. Hopefully, Silver
would go home, followed by Murphy and Blue, but
they didn't look like they were going to move from the
spot where we left them, maybe they knew we were
heading into danger and were not happy about it.
We suddenly spotted lights in the trees and as we
moved closer we realized there were lanterns hanging
from the branches guiding us down a path, we
stopped walking, but the shadow wolf kept going, I
turned to Nick and Marigold and pointed to my right
and nodded. They both smiled, it was time to start our
plan.
We had agreed once we got close enough we would
split up, so they had a better chance to rescue the
others as I distracted Caleb with the decoy jewel.
I knew the others were in the direction I had pointed,
as I could sense Tristan's mind link, but I didn't talk to
him as I had to concentrate on our plan. It was up to
Marigold now, before splitting up she had agreed to
fly ahead in her fairy form to make sure there weren't
any traps for us ahead.
"Right time for me to go." She said.
There was a flash of gold light as she shrank down to

butterfly size, she waved at us both with her tiny hands then flew off in the direction I had pointed.
"Wow, cute." Whispered Nick.
I smiled but before I could comment, Marigold was already flying back towards us.
"The others look alright but they are behind a magic barrier so you will have to distract Caleb a bit longer while I take it down, it shouldn't be a problem with my magic. Also, Finn and a few shadow demons are waiting too." She explained quietly, and then changed back into her human form.
"Right lets go." Said Nick.
"Once the barrier is ready to go down we will give you a signal." Said Marigold.
I nodded and watched them both move through the trees to the right.
I took a deep breath, put the real jewel back in my pocket and followed the path that was lit up; there was a clearing up ahead where Caleb was waiting. He patted the shadow wolf on the head and looked up.
"Ah, well done my pet I see you have brought us our special guest, come closer don't be shy." He said.
I walked out into the clearing and spotted the others behind the magical barrier Marigold had mentioned.
"No, Rose, why did you come?" Said Odin.
"You idiot!" Shouted Edmund and Tristan roared.
"Now now, that's no way to talk to the one who is here to save you." Said Finn who was sat near the others with a pile of weapons he must have taken from them, he smirked at me, but I ignored him and looked at the others.
Everyone looked alright, a few were covered in bruises and cuts from fighting, but it didn't look serious. Tristan was still in panther form, and he was pacing up and down angrily, Clover and Hannah were

holding hands and it looked like they had been crying and the others had a mixture of anger and fear on their faces. I also looked at the barrier they were in, it looked like the dome I had made before to protect the village, but I don't think the dome they were in was made to protect them it had a dark tinge to it and there was also magical runes on the ground around the barrier which was probably how Caleb and Finn had made it, I just hoped Marigold could break it with her magic.

"Is everyone alright?" I asked them.

A few of them nodded and Odin said, "We are fine please leave."

"Yeah, we are just having a rest inside this bubble." Said Edmund.

I smiled at them then turned back to Caleb, I was angry, but I knew I had to stay calm for the plan to work.

"I have brought you the thing you want most so let everyone else go." I said.

Finn laughed and Caleb said, "That will only happen once I have the jewel of darkness in my hands."

I looked back at my family and friends and saw pain, concern, and fear in their eyes.

"Rose don't you dare give them the jewel." Said Tristan who finally spoke through our mind link.

I looked at him and replied, **"I don't have much of a choice."**

"If you do this my brother would have died for nothing." His green eyes were full of pain, but I couldn't risk telling him the plan, I was afraid Caleb would somehow hear me, and for it to work I needed Caleb to believe he had won.

I spotted something behind the barrier it was Nick hiding behind a tree he put his thumbs up and nodded, it was time to start our plan.

The Magical Jewel, A Mystical Knight Novel, Book 1.
By Jade Stephenson ©.

"I'm sorry Tristan."
I turned back to Caleb and said aloud, "You promise no harm will come to them if I give you the jewel."
Caleb smiled and put his hand to his heart, "I give you my word love."
"Alright it's a deal." I said.
"Rose no, don't do it!" Shouted Odin.
I turned to them and shouted, "Shut up, I never asked for this. I hate magic, it's brought me nothing but pain. If you were my real friends you would understand my feelings and respect my decision. And the jewel will be better with him, right Caleb?"
"Yes Rose, everything will be better once I have the jewel." He smiled.
I sensed that Nick and Marigold was closer to the barrier, so I took the fake jewel from around my neck, cut my finger with the tip of my sword to draw blood onto it and then I made the jewel float towards Caleb with my magic, it glowed blue which helped make it look real. I glanced behind the barrier and prayed this plan would work.
Caleb took the jewel in his hands and laughed, "Thank you Rose, I have waited a long time for this." Before he noticed the jewel was a fake, I said, "Now it's your turn, let everyone go."
Caleb looked at me and then looked at the others but then a crazy look appeared on his face.
"I will let your family go but the Mystical Knights have caused me too much trouble, I will have to destroy them, I think it's time I try out my new magic."
He raised his hand up in the air and pointed it at the barrier and laughed.
Nothing happened, Caleb glanced at the jewel and tried again, still nothing happened. I glanced again behind the barrier and saw Marigold and Nick put their swords up in the air, they were ready.

I stopped the flow of magic in the fake jewel, the light vanished, and it turned black.

"What's wrong, why isn't it working?" Caleb shouted looking confused.

I smiled and winked at the others; Caleb noticed and looked again at the jewel in his hands.

"This is fake, but how?" He said.

"Oh, I'm sorry did you want the real thing? Ah I think I left it back at home." I laughed.

"Brilliant!" Shouted Edmund and the others laughed.

Caleb threw the fake jewel to the floor and shouted,

"Tricking me was the last thing you will ever do, and your friends will pay the price."

Shadow demons appeared all around him, but I smiled and said,

"Sorry but it's time we all went home."

The magic barrier disappeared; the others were free. Marigold and Nick ran out into the clearing with their weapons in hand, ready for a fight. As Finn was distracted Edmund charged at him and knocked him unconscious, the Mystical Knights got their weapons back.

"Nooooooo!" Yelled Caleb and the shadow demons attacked.

I held my sword up and defended myself from their attacks, I glanced beside me and noticed the Mystical Knights were doing the same and they were also protecting the Unicorn members, Anthony was also using a dagger to help defend the others, they were alright.

More shadows appeared in front of me, and I fought back using my sword only, as I was afraid to use my magic, I still felt weak even fighting with my sword was tiring me out. I stepped back from an attack but suddenly fell backwards over a tree root and the demon lunged and scratched my face, I yelled out in

pain then pushed the demon away with my sword.
Tristan pounced onto the demon and took it out; it
vanished in a puff of black smoke. Odin quickly pulled
me up back onto my feet.
"Rose are you alright?" He asked.
"Yes sorry, I guess I need more practice." I replied, as
I wiped the blood from my face.
Tristan stood beside me and growled at Caleb; he
had been stood watching us. Caleb smirked and said,
"Have you forgotten? I have another magic I can use
to hurt your friends."
He raised his hand up again and I saw something
sparkle on one of his fingers, my heart skipped a beat
as I realized it was Edmund's fire ring he must have
stolen it from him when he was caught, and that was
why I hadn't seen any fire balls when we were
fighting. Caleb winked at me and pointed his finger
towards the others who were still fighting shadow
demons.
"No!" I screamed, but it was too late, red flames shot
towards my family and friends.
The jewel of darkness reacted at my anger, it floated
out of my pocket and hovered in front of me, and I
rose up into the air a few inches off the ground as my
magic swirled around me. Then flames shot out from
the jewel and headed towards Caleb, but they weren't
red flames they were black.
There was a flash of bright light as the dark flames hit
its target and I landed back onto my feet. I looked to
my right and saw everyone was behind a wall of
water; Marigold had saved them just in time. They
were all looking at me with concern. Another man
suddenly appeared next to Finn wearing a black
cloak, he grabbed him and took him through a dark
portal but before they vanished I heard Finn shout.
"I will never forgive you for killing him, you will pay for

this!"

The rest of the shadow demons also disappeared, what did he mean? I wondered, as I looked towards Caleb, but he had also gone.

Odin was stood where Caleb had been, looking down at a pile of ash, he bent down and picked something up, it was Edmund's ring, he held it up for us to see then said, "Caleb is dead."

The jewel of darkness fell to the ground then I collapsed.

Chapter 21.
Family and Friends.

My eyes flickered open, and I saw light, I felt the warmth of someone holding my hand. I looked beside me and saw Odin sitting in the chair beside my bed, he had his eyes closed and it looked like he was praying.

"Don't worry, I'm not dead yet." I said and squeezed his hand.

"Rose you're awake." Said Isabella who was standing near the window I smiled at her and pushed myself up into a sitting position, the room spun, and I started to cough.

"Easy Rose you haven't fully recovered." Said Odin with concern and he handed me a glass of water.

I took a sip and looked around the room, I was in my bedroom at Old house and Odin and Isabella were the only ones here with me. I also noticed a drip in my arm pumping fluids into my body. As I drank I started to remember what had happened in the forest, I had used my magic with anger and now someone was dead, I killed him.

Caleb was dead because of me.

"I'm sorry.....I never meant to......I killed him." Tears welled up in my eyes.

Odin pulled me into a hug.

"Now that's enough, you have nothing to apologize for, it wasn't your fault, sometimes magic is unpredictable, and you can't fix what happened, it was Caleb's fault he should have known better. The jewel of darkness has chosen you to bear it, no one else can use it now, and that is not a bad thing, I would rather you have it then anyone else who would use it for bad things. I trust you can keep it safe and

control it, you did save us after all." He said.
He smiled, touched the bandage on my cheek and
looked carefully at my eyes he then got up and took
the glass out of my hand and said.
"I will go get you some more water."
Then he left the room but something about the way he
looked at me made me feel nervous, I looked at
Isabella and asked,
"Is there something wrong?"
"You used a lot of magic and some of it was dark
magic, sometimes doing that can change your
appearance, but don't worry it's already wearing off."
She came and sat on the end of my bed and handed
me my mirror.
I saw my reflection and gasped, my eyes had
changed color from brown to red.
**"You did well Rose, don't worry everything will be
alright."** Said Lucas who I could also see in the
mirror, I smiled at him then put the mirror down, my
eyes looked scary, even to me.
"Is everyone else alright?" I asked.
"Don't worry they're fine they are all just worried about
you, you have been asleep for three days." She
explained.
"Wow really, sorry I made everyone worry."
"It's alright we all know using magic can be hard on
your body and about your eyes they have already
faded down from that night so I'm sure you will have
brown eyes again soon. And don't mind Odin he was
just really worried about you, he has a daughter about
your age, and I think you remind him of her, if she
was still a human I think you would look alike too.
Even though you have not known each other for very
long I think Odin has started to treat you like his own
daughter he has grown fond of you, so for his sake
please be more careful."

"I will try…. Wait what do you mean about his daughter not being human?" I asked looking confused.

"Odin's daughter is a wolf; it's complicated I'm sure he will tell you all about it another time. For now, you should rest and remember we are not just Mystical Knights we are your friends and maybe in time we will become your second family. I won't lie to you, your life is going to change, and it won't be easy, but we will all be here for you, every step of the way." Smiled Isabella.

"Babysitting me won't be easy, are you sure you can all manage?" I laughed.

"Trust me, looking after you will be easy compared to Tristan and Edmund, those boys drive me crazy."

We both started laughing and we could not stop, it got worse when Odin came back into the room followed by the other Mystical Knights. They were all giving us funny looks as they tried to work out what we were laughing at, so of course that made us laugh harder. We managed to stop as Hannah ran into the room followed by Spencer the dog, they both jumped onto the bed and Hannah gave me a hug as she shouted, "Great, you're alright!"

The other Unicorn members entered the room and smiled at me. I wiped the tears from my eyes and smiled back, I knew then that Lucas was right, as I looked at all the smiling faces in the room; I knew everything would be alright.

Chapter 22.
1 Month Later.

It was time for the Mystical Knights to leave and head home to Sunlight City. One month has passed since the events in Dark Forest with Caleb and the shadow demons and nothing else has happened since, no one else has tried to take the jewel of darkness from me and Finn has not returned as we feared he would. I was standing under the Willow tree I had helped grow, watching the Mystical Knights pack up their saddle bags and get their horses ready for the ride home with a sadness I did not expect to feel. We had all grown closer over the many weeks living together, Isabella was right I did think of them as my second family now, and I would miss them.

I was supposed to go with them as by law anyone with a strong magical item or ability has to move to Sunlight City so the Mystical Knights can protect them, but I wasn't ready yet to leave my home or family at Unicorn Stables. So Odin got special permission off the shapeshifter king, Eric Hart, to allow me to stay at home longer until I am ready to leave, they have also given me the keys to Old house so I can keep studying magic and keep practicing my sword techniques without having to disturb the Unicorn Stable members, even though they have all become better friends with the Mystical Knights they still don't trust magic but they have let me move back into the house with them so I can live with them for one more year, before moving to Sunlight City.

The only condition of letting me stay at home for one more year is that I can't use my magic, the king doesn't want to risk me hurting myself or anyone else with my magic and he doesn't want me using magic

without a Mystical Knight present, so he has banned
me from using it while I am living at Greenfield village.
I can only learn about magic by reading the books
Odin is leaving at Old house for me.

I looked down at the device around my arm and
sighed, it was a metal band that would let the Mystical
Knights know if I used magic and if I did I would have
no choice a Mystical Knight would come and escort
me to Sunlight City, it also blocks me from using
magic by stopping the flow of magic entering my body
and makes me unable to use it so I would struggle
even if I tried. The only way it could be removed from
my arm was by a pass code only a Mystical Knight
would know. It was called a Magic Repel.
I was not happy when Odin had given it to me, it had
felt like they didn't trust me, but he explained he had
no choice and when I saw the tears in his eyes as he
placed it onto my arm I forgave him, it was the kings
rule after all, and I have lived without using magic
before, so I'm sure I can manage. And I could not stay
mad at Odin he had become the father I never had.

A hand reached out and touched my arm above the
Magic Repel, I looked up and saw big green eyes
looking at me.
"Are you alright Rose?" Asked Tristan.
I smiled and nodded, "Are you ready to leave?"
"Yes, but before I go I have something to give you."
He said and took hold of my hand; he attached
something to my bracelet.
I looked down and saw a little wooden black panther
charm with green eyes painted on it.
"My brother made it for me a long time ago, but I
added the green eyes, Lucas had said when you feel
lonely it will remind you you're not alone." Said

Tristan.

"If Lucas made it for you then you should keep it." I said.

"No, it's alright I have plenty of animals he made at home, and I think Lucas would want you to have it."

"Thank you, I love it." I smiled.

"My brother would be glad to hear that." Tristan smiled back.

"We are all ready to leave now." Said Odin and he came to stand beside us with the other Mystical Knights. He held out a box he had in his hands.

"This is for you Rose, from all of us, all Mystical Knights receive one when they join us."

"Um, but I'm not a Mystical Knight."

"Well maybe not officially but we have been training you and once you do come and live with us I'm sure you will become one, you told Marigold you wanted to be one of us, right?" Said Odin with a big smile on his face.

I took the box from him and opened it up, inside was the most beautiful dagger I had ever seen. It had jewels around the pommel but what I loved the most was the silver horse etched onto the grip of the handle and on the blade it read, 'We spread the message of magic, unity, harmony and hope for a better world.' It was the Mystical Knights motto. I shut the box and jumped onto Odin to give him a hug.

"Thank you." I shouted.

"Well, I'm glad you like it." Laughed Odin.

The other Mystical Knights laughed too as I gave them all a hug.

Odin put his hand on my cheek and smiled, the bandage was long gone but I still have a scar where the shadow had scratched my face. I'm just glad my eyes were brown again.

"Well, I think it's time for us to leave, I want you to

remember everything we have told you and keep practicing with your weapons but please be careful. We will miss you Rose, please keep in touch." Said Odin.

I nodded and placed a hand onto the S.C.D. attached to my belt the Mystical Knights had given me, luckily the Magic Repel did not affect me using it, as anyone who has used magic in the past can use it, so I would definitely be using this to keep in touch with them.

We all said our goodbyes as the Mystical Knights mounted their horses and I stood with Silver and waved goodbye as one by one they rode off back into Dark Forest to get back onto the road that would take them home.

I was worried what the future would bring but as I stood and patted Silver on the neck, I smiled knowing everything would be alright because I am not alone.

****

Behind Rose and Silver, a boy is standing behind a tree, he is also watching the Mystical Knights leave, with a smile on his face.

"The time is not yet upon us Finn." Said Ash Greenweed the dark fairy.

"Yes, I know." Said Finn.

They both turn around and leave through a dark portal.

The End.

The Magical Jewel, A Mystical Knight Novel, Book 1.
By Jade Stephenson ©.

******

Author's Notes.

Writing this book was difficult for me as I have always struggled to get ideas and words out of my head to write on paper, but I have had this story in my head for a long time, so I really wanted to try my best to finally write the full book. I also love reading stories and looking at all the different types of books you can get when I visit book shops and hoping one day I will see my book on the shelf.
So, if you have a story in your head but like me you find it difficult, just remember to write all you can and never give up because one day your dream might come true, and I could be reading your book one day too.

I would like to dedicate this book to my wonderful family and to all the Animals of the world.
I would also like to dedicate this book to the RDA Unicorn Centre in Hemlington, Middlesbrough. A wonderful place where I did an NVQ Level 1 and 2 in horse care, I learnt everything I know about horses there and met some amazing people and horses. It is a charity and also a great place for disabled and non-disabled people to learn how to ride horses so if you can please donate at
https://www.rdaunicorncentre.co.uk. Thank you.

To my dearest readers, thank you for reading my book and please help whenever and wherever you can, abused and abandoned animals everywhere await your love and assistance. xxx

Printed in Great Britain
by Amazon

21808813R00111